ASCENSION TO DEATH

Published in 2018 by
HAUS PUBLISHING LTD
4 Cinnamon Row
London SW11 3TW

Originally published in Arabic as *Mi'raj al-mawt* by Mamdouh Azzam
Copyright © 2018 Mamdouh Azzam
Translation Copyright © 2018 Max Weiss

A CIP catalogue record for this book is available from the British Library

ISBN: 978-1-910376-36-2
eISBN: 978-1-910376-37-9

Typeset in Garamond by MacGuru Ltd

Printed in Spain by Liberdúplex

ASCENSION TO DEATH

MAMDOUH AZZAM

Translated by
Max Weiss

MAMDOUH AZZAM is a Syrian novelist. His most celebrated and controversial novel is *The Palace of Rain*, a powerful and daring treatment of taboos in Syria's conservative Druze religion and community. *Ascension to Death* was first published in Arabic as *Mi'raj al-mawt*, and was adapted into the award-winning film *Al-Lajat*, directed by Riyad Shayya.

Will I leave nothing behind on earth
when I pass on?
Flowers at least?
Anthems at least?
What will my heart do?
Or did I come to this earth for nothing?
– Aztec sung poetry

Play on! My dreams of youth may now be gone. Still
time drags along…
– Abu al-'Ala' al-Ma'arri

1

The Captive

In the morning she began to cough up blood. For the first time in a month, ever since they had brought her to this room and bolted the door, she felt her joints softening, her body, dry and light, starting to sag, no longer able to hold up her weak and weary head.

She wasn't hungry either – this, too, for the first time – finding that the scraps left behind in the dish in front of her gave off a nauseating, putrid stench of uncooked food. It was the smell of her own blood.

She couldn't see a thing. The room was cramped and dark. The only light was seeping through cracks in the wooden shutters.

In the beginning, when she had been so overwhelmed with nausea that she fell over, sweat caking her clothes with the musty stench of pus, she had thought that her dinner had gone bad simply because she had taken so long to eat it (she couldn't see the food anyway, so taste became her only way to figure out what it was). She had come to believe that darkness was all there had ever been, forgetting that just two weeks earlier she had been able to see perfectly well, once her eyes had adjusted to the gloom. But her vision had grown weaker over the past week, and she could no longer make out anything more than a thin film, as if her eyes were coated in mist. She started hallucinating. It was like a dream: a rising column of haggard birds, black and white roses entwined, radiance, curling smoke, materialising right there in front of her against a geometric background of stone tiles – occasionally they would shimmer, when the faint oscillating rays of light slipped through the cracks and shone upon them, but at other times they seemed to merge into continuous dark cement.

They had locked her away in the only storehouse in the entire village. It was a well-known fact that her grandfather had built it when he first arrived from Anatolia, fleeing the Ottoman army. He constructed the building with a small window that could easily be concealed by piling up rubbish and manure outside. The door wasn't easy to find either, an opening less than a metre wide, in a neglected corner on the ground floor. For some reason no one could now recall, they called the storehouse 'the horse shed'.

The old women monitoring her captivity dumped all the manure and garbage outside by the window. They swept the place thoroughly, fertilised the soil and planted mint, watering it every day. They didn't want her to die too quickly, though, so one of the old women forced open a crack in the windowsill with a knife she had brought without letting her two spinster sisters know and spent the rest of the day convinced she had done a good deed.

The old ladies were oddly transformed by Salma's arrival, as if they had been exhumed from swamps in which they had been buried, brought out of their perpetual spinsterhood and rejuvenated by a cascade of extraordinary changes. Life pulsed through them; like lionesses, they came back into the world. They scrubbed away the stinking filth of manure, picking through each other's hair in search of ticks, and then put on their finest clothes, which had long been stored away. They had dug a pit in the ground near the storehouse window. Stopping there had become part of their sacred ritual of going out.

The window faced west, out on to the sheep pen that had been constructed on a high rocky outcrop that towered over the desolate valley. From outside it looked like a palace, standing tall with its thick walls. This was why Salma had never tried, not even once, to climb up to the window and shout for help. Once she had heard the bleating of the sheep and the lowing of the huge Damascus cows, she was sure that nobody would hear her cries. She knew exactly where she was. During the first few days she tried to reach the upper opening, climbing the wall numerous times and pounding on the thick, blackened wood with her fists.

The old ladies must have heard something, and their brother, who was there at the time, winked at them. They knew what they had to do. They had seen their mother do it many times before while their father had been in hiding, when they heard the boom of Ottoman artillery or, much later, the crack of French rifles. They filled two canvas sacks with wheat and stacked them in front of the opening, covering them with cloth made out of goat's hair.

After doing this they realised they wouldn't be able to hear any cries for help, so whenever they were home alone they would press their ears against the wall, and something like a distant heartbeat would reach them, as if from deep inside the earth, sending the strangest kind of ecstasy through their withered bodies.

Eventually, when they could no longer make out the buried palpitations, they stopped listening. Sorrow began to eat away at them, bit by bit; their lives descended into the depths of crushing boredom, only ever disrupted when they prepared Salma's daily meal and then dropped it down to her. It was as if the rhythm of those cries for help rising out of the storehouse below them had become mixed up in their ears with the echoes of their own beating hearts. Meanwhile, Salma's will faltered. On the first day of her third week there she tried to climb up the rubble to reach the window. She failed. She never tried again after that, even though she wanted to. Suddenly she had trouble breathing – it felt like she was suffocating – so she clambered up the side where the window was and sucked down some air through the crack and the narrow slits. The mint refreshed her a bit, but she couldn't hold herself up. Her hand slipped; she lost her grip and fell to the ground.

She felt perpetually groggy. She didn't sleep. She suffered fits of agitation that made her hallucinate: a gelatinous dreamland, starry visions, a flock of birds uproarious in song, fish swimming through a flood of ivory water.

All she had left was memory. In every moment the

pathways of her memory were bright, scorching; nothing could stop her from thinking back to happier times. She lay on her back in fields of memory for long stretches of time, floating through the luminous expanses of her long-gone happiness, plummeting into the carefree space of idle hours, unaffected by the passage of time. She would only move to adjust her body, rubbed raw by the thread-bare mattress.

As the days dragged on she started to eat her meals much more slowly. In general, they consisted of little more than a piece of flatbread and a few olives or a hunk of cheese. Her aunts would toss the food at her wrapped in a cloth. She didn't know it was a piece of her own clothing. They had shredded two of her dresses and then used the scraps to tie together her disgusting daily meal, throwing it down her way just before midnight, as if none of them wanted to see her up close for fear that they might be ambushed by compassion. Even so, they couldn't help but mutter an expression of sympathy and mercy whenever it was their turn to hurl the food at her. She might hear them let out a sigh, sincere and tinged with grief, but it never went beyond that, and they certainly never considered saving her from the clutches of imminent death. On the contrary, they became experts in making her disgusting daily meal, concocting something new each and every time.

It energised their work, helped them to get through their pointless days, injected meaning into their empty lives. Once Salma quit her pounding, the rhythm of life that had suddenly been awakened in them ceased and cooking took up all their time.

Once in a while they might add a spoonful of sugar to the bread, include a mouldy piece of Turkish delight or a shard of crispbread, some *mujaddara* or a tomato. Whenever Umm Mut'ib brought them a slab of molasses and some sesame halva, they didn't say a word; knowing full well that she had brought it for Salma, they ate it all before setting off to cook a meal for themselves with the enthusiasm of new-world explorers. In the evening they threw Salma enough nauseating halva to bring down a cow. Her situation was a flashpoint of discussion, debate and disagreement. In the end, though, they would resist every fresh idea in silent and reasoned agreement, recognising full well what that meant. The fact that they were merely prolonging her life wasn't lost on them. But they were all thinking the exact same thing: if Salma died, what would they have left but that meaningless rot at the core of their empty lives?

Salma's last night was a long one. She was unable to fall asleep. The idea of death, cloaked in tatters, was lodged in her mind. In the evening she came down with a slight fever, and she awoke after sleeping the whole day through, exhausted, unable to get up, worn out by feelings of despair and misery. The sudden fever terrified her. Trembling and afraid, she sat straight up on her mattress, watching her twenty years as they leaked out of her drop by drop. Abd al-Kareem came into her mind, and she tried to spark her memory with the longing of desire. She saw him at first as an apparition in the murky darkness, an infinitesimal shadow, elongated, floating like a fish, deep in discussion with a giant mass of other featureless forms.

This vision of him sparked her memory. Just then, searing images from the past came flooding back, revealing everything to her: the months of passionate love, travels together adorned with the silver lining of happiness, ships of wonder, days, hours, minutes spent together, Abd al-Kareem's face, his words. For hours she imagined him standing right there in front of her, talking to her as he stroked his stubbly chin, hunched over like a letter of the alphabet. This time he looked radiant, about to burst with a mysterious secret, bathed in a kind of joy she only rarely saw in him. She called out to him. He didn't reply. She called out to him as loud as she could, imagining he should be able to hear her even if he had been crouching behind a curtain, but he didn't respond. What she didn't realise was that her voice hadn't even come out of her throat at all. She had lost the power of speech. Even so, she found it strange that her voice wouldn't travel very far at night. She was astonished by this failure, broken, gazing at her beautiful apparition in the translucent light as it dissolved into dawn.

Her vision evaporated amid the cacophony of overlapping morning sounds: the bleating of sheep, the lowing of cattle, the shepherd shouting in the courtyard, the coughing of early risers, the crowing of the cock. She couldn't understand what she was hearing and seeing. Then she started to feel cold, suddenly stricken with nausea, as her veins bled, her rational mind subsided and scattered into the stony air of the sealed room. Meanwhile, her body fell apart, even as it imagined itself to be on the brink of deliverance.

In the morning she began to swim through the haze of a deep and foggy slumber, bathed in tranquillity. She coughed lightly and began to spit up bile, which quickly turned red. In that moment she saw that everything around her was transparent and clearly visible; she felt as if she were being lifted on a stretcher made of air until she believed her very existence, the room and the silent darkness, the soft light coming in through the crack in the shutter, were nothing but tricks of the mind that had never existed at all.

Now her death was at hand.

2

The Bereft

Like a madman, stricken with panic and convulsions, trapped in a fevered frenzy, Abd al-Kareem spent days searching for her, questioning people throughout the village, asking and asking over and over again. He bared his soul to everyone, sharing his sadness that was mixed with a strange kind of yearning and camouflaged in an incandescent glow. He found nothing but dejection, dead ends and disappointment.

His questions ceased to have any meaning. Everyone glared at him. It was as if they were refusing to recognise the basic fact that Salma had once existed in the village.

Even his own mother, who had heard the whole story more or less from Umm Mut'ib, wouldn't tell him anything. Much later, after he had left the village and emigrated to Brazil, she would say, 'We aren't in the same league as the Zeebs.'

She was worried he might be attacked by some thug or by Salma's entire family. Despite the fact that she harboured bitterness like the coppery taste of blood in her mouth, weeping whenever she saw him come home late at night exhausted, destroyed by the burning in his heart, she kept silent. She cried so hard she gave herself chronic migraines, which led her to start wrapping her head in a black mourning-band, wound so tightly around her skull that it nearly cracked. Meanwhile, he pushed ahead in his search, indefatigable, perpetually fixated on his unchanging questions: 'Have you seen her?' 'Do you know anything?' 'Where have they taken her?' The whole time he was searching for her, as if he were on a sacred journey, he never spoke about anything else. He would grab anyone he happened to pass by, squeeze their arms forcefully and demand, 'Have you seen her?'

Once he went around asking every single guest at a wedding party, his lips turning blue as he pronounced the same tired words with calculated precision. His drowsy eyes were vacant, devoid of any light, and he was crushed when they responded to him with nothing but disdain.

Fate was no help either. It seemed to be conspiring against him instead. One night his father suddenly came down with a strange illness and collapsed without warning. Bed-ridden, he recovered in steely silence. Then they moved him to the hospital. When the doctor told them there didn't seem to be anything wrong with him, the house was filled with a kind of bewilderment that spared nobody.

Whenever he looked in on him, his father refused to turn away his piercing, fiery eyes, wide open, unblinking, expressing an anxious curiosity that Abd al-Kareem had never seen in him before. Only his mother understood why. He was increasingly uncertain whether the

Zeebs would allow Abd al-Kareem to remain alive. Their assault had stunned him. Their brutality had struck fear in his weakened heart. The panic in his eyes didn't go away until his wife whispered the news of Salma's death in his ear. At that point his dread dissipated, and he enjoyed a moment's peace. But the sickness persisted.

Abd al-Kareem was frightened by his father's continued inability to speak. It was as if Abd al-Kareem's devastated soul was now being covered in hard and muddy sorrow. He couldn't do anything. Every moment of Salma's disappearance deepened his sadness, his fear of what the Zeebs might do to his family, his concern for what little money he had to offer them to keep the threat of poverty at bay. With all the disrespect that people were showing him, there was little more for him to do than fade away. He became a ghost, condensed into a cloud. His brother Salman told him he was going to have a breakdown if he carried on like this. Behind his back many people in the village said the same thing. He was constantly on the move, wandering around in circles. He asked strangely invasive questions about Salma with a volatile tenacity resembling the nature of an unstable chemical compound about to ignite. Every day his demeanour became more and more susceptible to collapse, but it didn't.

Everybody knew that the one person holding him together was his mother, once she had understood that her son had come back to her as a child. His childhood had always enchanted her. Despite the fact that she had given birth to three other boys and two girls, her heart was unequivocally inclined towards him. She had never dared lay a hand on him – 'I just can't,' she would say, even as she chased after one of his brothers with a stick or threw whatever was in her hand at the rest of them whenever she got upset. She had always been severe with the other children, right from the start, barking orders at them as she sat down to milk the cow in the evening – looking like a proud and solemn statue, unmoving against a background of unceasing chaos – or reclining beneath the giant eucalyptus tree that had been planted more than forty years before, as she somehow managed to hum a tune and order people about at the same time.

Some had believed that this bitter old woman was never going to experience love again, so they couldn't believe their eyes when she broke out of her dark mood and started to look after Abd al-Kareem. Her eyes pooled with warmth – like the sea, churned by the tide of a heavy heart. Her face turned pale, as if she were meeting her son for the first time. The love that suddenly washed across her face, like a high curling wave, drove her wild.

Although she seemed prepared to carry on that way indefinitely, it didn't last long. Abd al-Kareem slowed down; his sense of urgency flagged. His manic activity gave way to slack stillness. He didn't come out of the house the following morning. Salma was truly dead to him, even though the Zeebs hid the news of her death from him and nobody ever told him what had happened. They buried her that night. One of her paternal uncles and three other men carried her down to the poppy field on the back of a donkey. They didn't bother holding a funeral, just wrapped her in a simple shroud and took her out to the valley road.

Abd al-Kareem's mother found out that afternoon. She had never cared for the girl, whom she believed had made many mistakes. She would never be able to forgive a married woman for leaving her husband to live with another man, even if that man happened to be her son. At first she felt like a heavy weight had been lifted from her shoulders, let out a sigh of relief and made no attempt to hide how pleased she was. But, years later, when she so desperately missed Abd al-Kareem, who was never coming back, she cried her eyes out when she learned how the Zeebs had treated their daughter. They had cut her hair, dressed her in her only gown and poisoned her. Salma's life had simply slipped away. She had been gone for ten hours before anyone noticed.

Late in the morning after Salma's death, ready to march behind Abd al-Kareem, she went into his room to find out what was taking him so long to get up. She found him laid out like a corpse under a blanket of bloated sorrow and longing for the departed. She nervously praised God and then cried for a long time.

In Abd al-Kareem's eyes everything seemed to blur, as though he were seeing things through a distant fog, concealed behind a veil: languid, gelatinous, supple. But that all ceased the night before Salma passed away, when the mare whinnied three long times to the north of the village. He had been sitting with Umm Samer on the small bench in front of her house as she gazed at him with a strange sadness that made him tremble.

'That poor girl,' she said, as his stomach knotted up. She beat her breast and let out a cry of anguish, then whispered, 'Go on and cry. Cry. You can.'

He couldn't understand anything she was saying. He stood up. All he wanted to do was get away from her.

She squeezed his hand and said, 'Come back. Go inside.'

He followed her into the house without knowing exactly what he was going to do. But she knew what she wanted. Throwing her powerful arms around his neck and pulling him in close, she curled up underneath him and started to kiss his neck, his face and his lips. She undid the buttons concealing her voluptuous chest and placed her breast in his mouth even as she went on kissing him. Just then, she shoved him away and darted over to lock the door before wheeling back around to continue undressing in a hurry.

The mare was still whinnying as he left. It wasn't until someone fired off three rounds in her direction that she finally quietened down. An emphatic silence spread over the place. Everything around him was illuminated, emerging from behind a translucent veil, out of the distant fog and the troubled atmosphere.

What had driven that whore to treat him like a schoolboy who still didn't know how to walk? And how could that flabby softness make her body seem so powerful? That poor woman. Why was she in mourning? Who was the dearly departed that inspired her lament?

Only then did he begin to see things as they really were.

He was shocked by the sight of the wintry village under the gauzy cover of darkness: bare, silent conical trees; the bray and the clip-clop of a donkey carting water from the well; an extraordinary mass of shimmering smoke that rose from the fireplaces to cascade over the horizon in the pale, soft glow; men huddled together in the doorways, resisting the end of their night. With the stench of that whore still clogging his nostrils, he felt short of breath, like somebody suddenly coming to after a deep slumber, and from deep down inside there arose a ringing in his ears, swaddled in feelings of filth, despair and hopelessness.

On his way back he ran into his brother, who grabbed him by the hand and said, 'Come with me.' Abd al-Kareem's brother seemed to know that something had happened. They saw three women coming from Parliament Road, staring enigmatically at the two of them.

'Don't you get it?' Abd al-Kareem's brother asked furiously. 'They've humiliated us!'

For the first time in a month, Abd al-Kareem spoke. 'And how far would you need to get away before you felt safe?'

For a moment, his brother regarded him in disbelief.

'Run a bath for me,' he ordered his mother once he was back home. 'That filthy woman has made me unclean,' he muttered to himself.

His mother didn't appear to hear what he said as she hurried to get some kindling to light the stove on the other side of the flimsy wall. She was in tears, repeating over and over, 'Oh, my son! My boy!' She was filled with joy, as the fields of happiness deep down inside her turned green and verdant.

When he climbed into bed, she tucked him in with a touch from her sacred world: verses from the *Kitab al-Hikma*, her pious devotion, rose water, sheets fit for a wedding night. Then she kneeled down beside his bed, watching his slow and regular breathing. Just then she believed she was witnessing his death. In the morning, after she woke him up, he told her about the dream he'd had in which he saw Salma's death. She was on a jagged mountain ledge surrounded by crags swept clean by a wintry gale, as flocks of yellowish vultures circled overhead to drag her towards a precipitous and plummeting abyss.

At this point his mother started exalting God. 'Praise be to you, my Lord! Praise be to you, my God!'

3

The Meddler

Sitt al-Husn's protest flew in the face of every conceivable piece of good advice.

She had woken early, which was unusual for her. She noticed that the cow was still in the pen and that the house reeked with the stench of filth and urine. Outside, the misty July dew clung to everything. Through the narrow window, nature appeared swollen, heavy with dusty gloom.

That was enough for her to intuit what had happened. She had never believed such a thing could take place. What had once brought solace to the deepest recesses of her mind, her imagination, now terrified her. She had been driven into a panic ever since Sayyah Zeeb came to see her one morning and uttered those portentous words, 'If anything happens to her, it'll be on your head.'

☾

When Abu Saeed had asked for her hand in marriage one winter's evening two years earlier, she had consented without hesitation. Long years of spinsterhood had weighed her down. Her meagre appetite had desiccated her body and her blood. She had often thought that her basket of dreams would never be filled. Her time had passed, her hopes unfulfilled, her dreams scattered. She had surrendered unconditionally to the judgement of time. She had given up, performing the mourning ritual of an old maid: reading coffee grounds. She knew it was a superstition, which was why she had never seen Abu Saeed, not even once, in the spindly traces inside the cup, its interlaced branches and interlocking pathways. His unexpected appearance was a happy ending for her dead-ened, miserable hope.

Abu Saeed didn't propose until fifteen years after his wife's death. Her stomach had grown bloated with water bubbles that were left untreated until a very advanced stage. The only doctor they consulted didn't have sufficient knowledge or medication to cure her. Her body broke down, and she died, leaving her husband with the respon-sibility for raising their only son. Saeed grew up in his father's shadow – weak, consumptive – but once he reached adolescence he became a different person. Emerging from a haze of laziness and decrepitude, he suddenly shook off the weight of despair that had been mercilessly pressing down upon him ever since childhood. The way that he transformed his reputation from that point on was simple enough: he only left the house in clean clothes that his aunt had pressed for him, his hair neatly combed, smooth as a snake, with spit-polished shoes. His gait changed, too, and he no longer loped along like a wounded dog, as Sitt al-Husn used to say, but peacocked around town instead. On a visit with his father to the shrine of John the Baptist, he bought a large bottle of cologne from one of the shops scattered around the Umayyad Mosque. It was a stroke of genius, as the pungent scent attracted half the young ladies in the village, and they showered him with tender kisses behind their houses, or in the outhouses and in the fields during springtime and harvest. This was how Saeed matured before his time, devouring everything in sight. His reputation as a boy soft as moss was replaced by the image of a fearless ladies' man no woman could resist.

There was a surprise lying in wait for Sitt al-Husn when she married Abu Saeed. The wedding preparations didn't last more than two days, during which she had been unable to see or get to know Saeed at all. By the time she finally met him, after they brought her home that night, he was coated in a lustre of kisses and barely acknowledged her presence. The young lady he was with clawed at him with ravenous desire. They fondled one another ecstatically while everyone else was enjoying the wedding. She spotted them in a darkened corner behind the house where they had absconded to be alone. The aroma of sweet clover in that weedy corner was intensified by the early-evening moisture. Needing to relieve herself, one of the women had directed her where to go, but she got mixed up in the darkness and suddenly found herself beside the two of them.

She loudly cleared her throat with no idea what might happen next. The young lady Saeed was with instinctively shut her eyes and recoiled.

Saeed calmly turned towards his father's future wife, who saw his penis erect in the moonlight like an ancient marble column. 'Hello there,' he said in a statuesque voice.

It mortified her. Neither one of them fully understood what had just happened. He didn't even realise that she was his father's wife until it was too late. She didn't recognise him until the next morning when he came to congratulate her. But a mere two hours later Sitt al-Husn had turned into a feral cat. The romantic scene had aroused her, filled her with voracious desire. So she surrendered herself completely to Abu Saeed when she discovered that the very same demon she saw in Saeed also lurked, breathless, in his gaunt, ageing body. She came twice. Early the next morning Abu Saeed was a crumpled heap, but she was a lioness in the jungle. When she finally fell asleep she dreamed she was plummeting from the top of a mountain, under attack by a green monster with quills like a porcupine. She woke up with a start. The room was shut, dark, even though the house was softly illuminated by spring light seeping in through the shutters. Through the small aperture at the front of the room she saw a flower bed in which oleanders were interspersed with damask rose and gillyflower bushes and three varieties of lilies. She was revived somewhat by the vibrant, colourful symphony, the effusion of sparrows and goldfinches. Still, she felt drained, unsettled by a vague sense of unease. Unable to keep herself from feeling depressed, she sought shelter in the spring sunshine, thinking she was alone. But she was ambushed by three women – Abu Saeed's sisters, it turned out – who came to greet her. Then she saw Saeed.

As he kissed her, she felt the blood rushing to her cheeks, her stomach boiling. She suddenly understood she was never going to be satisfied.

Heavy rains fell that year, putting an end to three years of drought and building a foundation of happiness for Sitt al-Husn: abundant wheat harvests; calving cows; a high price for the ewes she had once purchased with gold bracelets; long, regular absences from Abu Saeed's house during the day; and luxurious hours of sleep that had recently brought her desire roaring back to life.

Saeed used to hang around the house. He had returned from his military service without any work, aspirations or plans. In that vacuous, groggy lethargy, he did little more than sleep and marinate in a mixture of laziness and Don Juanism – unhinged desire flashed in his eyes.

His father was none too pleased about his son going out to work in the fields. Ever since his first wife died he had been satisfied with the one son he had been granted by the tree of life, and he always guarded him against any hardship. He was content to watch his son's development, his torpor and hopes creeping along like vines. He would gaze at him before heading off to work. As he watched his pliable body steadily mature, he pitied him but was also satisfied by the nourishment of his life. By the time Saeed had grown up, habit had become an unbreakable tradition. Abu Saeed would never know that this very same tradition, which had taken root under his own roof, was the towering tree of fornication flowering with the fruit of death.

One morning the two of them had breakfast together.

When she asked him how the food tasted, he said he liked all of it: eggs with butter and yoghurt and onion. The variety reminded him of the pleasure that comes when the first hint of spring hits the air. He talked to her about his time in the army. (His father had neglected to submit a statement attesting that he was an only child, and it took sixty days for the matter to be sorted out, for the legal papers to be corrected in the military bureaucracy.)

He said that eating was restricted to a few minutes for each meal. And, day after day, a human being would lose every sign of individuality as he was transformed into an automaton no different from all the others. No personal desires, no tastes, no food requests, no appetite whatsoever. The company of women was prohibited, even though they were what interested the soldiers most. He whispered to her that, for him, being denied women for two months was like being separated from life. He paid no attention to the blood rushing to her cheeks and launched into a boastful monologue about some marginal, idiotic adventures, wars he waged, a life grounded in love. He was a dreamer, sculpting stories out of his words of clay. He somehow knit the stories together into a colourful skein, disorienting as it may have been with all its ins and outs and knots. In this he seemed to be pulling out a cloth from inside of himself in which to wrap Sitt al-Husn, to hold her down so that she would be unable to move a muscle. He was like a tiger – playful, curious, no longer possessing the will to suppress his desire, coiled and ready to pounce in any direction. At her, to be precise. In the maelstrom of his lust, he forgot that she was related to him. And, to her astonishment, she forgot that she was old enough to be his mother. The only thing that interrupted the scorching flow of her forbidden passion was the footfalls on the grass of the donkey, and, further behind, Abu Saeed collapsing from exhaustion. She ran over to grab the reins, guiding the donkey into the pen, an obedient woman overcome with crushing feelings of shame.

Those feelings didn't last long. She gave them up, vaporised them in the love that carried her away like a moth to a flame. Abu Saeed was so oblivious that she was able to act freely, though. There was something kind and innocent about him, which meant that if things got complicated, as they did on numerous occasions, he would have no idea what was going on. As far as he was concerned, her fawning interest in Saeed seemed like attentive mothering. She never stopped showing him signs of respect, and, to his simple mind, this was a beautiful sentiment, one he could also enjoy because of his own vigorous masculinity.

That wasn't what encouraged her the most, however. She experienced the fullness of a flowering tree, an almost feline desire. Saeed didn't leave her side once during their three days of sexual delight. They addressed each other like lovers in a private paradise. Even her giggle oozed with flaming passion. She radiated vitality into his arid life. When she sat down in front of him, her white thighs struck him like thunder, like a breath of fresh air. He feigned indifference. He knew all about the ancient wiles of women, which he had stopped thinking about as soon as he discovered them. He was drained. Her fiery advances helped bring him back to his senses. At first those initial steps felt like suicide. He was lashed to the ligaments of his desire. Soon his resistance started to break down. Her harshness with him began to soften and then, finally, disappear.

The events that followed amounted to a diabolical scheme that benefited them both. State security had arrested Shafiq Khalil and a few young men from some other villages after pamphlets critical of the regime had been distributed throughout the local area. It was the talk of the village for several days. Everyone concealed their sympathy and instead they mustered up uncommon bravery to feign their horror at what those men had done. Abu Shafiq dropped by the house and told Abu Saeed, 'Brother-in-law, you're the only one who can help me.'

Abu Saeed's sister was married to a high-ranking army officer who lived in Damascus, and they went to see him.

Sitt al-Husn didn't hide her joy, but she was also deeply concerned by the nagging sense that it was getting late and Saeed still wasn't back yet. He had left before his father, didn't show up for lunch, and now the sun had disappeared without his return.

After dinner she saw the lantern light in his room was still unlit. This didn't bother her too much, though. She was a patient person who was very good at waiting. Intuitively she knew that he wanted to run away. She never let that get to her, however, because she would never give him the chance.

Except for a few stray dogs, the village drifted off to sleep. Low clouds deflected the moonlight into corridors in the sky. Just before midnight, wolves howled in the foothills.

A few minutes later there were faint, tentative taps at Saeed's door. He had been awake, waiting. For the first time in his life he was trembling. His teeth chattered together violently. When he opened the door his face looked sorrowful and exhausted. All he could do was smile.

'Everything all right?' he asked, sensing the absurdity of the question. He leaned towards her, as if he were about to embrace the aroused woman standing there in front of him. It was precisely this sort of absurdity that brought men and women together time after time.

'I'm scared,' she whispered. 'Those howling wolves frightened me.'

'The ones up in the foothills?'

'Yes. Listen.'

She stepped inside without hesitation, closing the door behind her. He turned the lamp on. Light flooded the room.

'Now why would you go and do that?' she asked, switching the light back off. 'Are we going to stay up? I want to sleep in here,' she purred suggestively as she sat on the edge of the bed unceremoniously.

Her words were like a warning. Her incendiary invitation, the tension in her slender fingers, her ample body in a nightgown, her eyes alight with the glow of desire – fire raced through his body, scorched by the heat of her arousal. He didn't sit beside her as her husband's son committing a forbidden act of love. He was neither lover nor beloved. He surrendered to the carnal fervour. It consumed his body, leaving the devastation of a cyclone in its wake.

Eventually they both gave in to the urges of their excited bodies: furtive kisses, playful caresses, secret words thick with desire. They seized the opportunity to violate every taboo, setting the stage for a complicated romance. Every day Sitt al-Husn's impetuousness grew, became more combustible, even as Saeed cooled off, quenched. He quit going into the village, put an end to the few inconsequential relationships he had with young women. After several months of being in love, he became thick and bloated, like a billy goat. Sitt al-Husn started coming to see him almost every day after Abu Saeed had left for work. They let all the breadwinning responsibilities fall on his shoulders while they indulged their infatuation. She would visit him at night during the summer harvest. When Abu Saeed went out into the fields, she would sneak into his room, press her nipples against his mouth while he was sleeping until he detected their sweet smell of ripe peaches. Then she would tear off his clothes with the force of an advancing army. Sitting there in the moonlight, she would start getting undressed, a powerful ritual that awakened their crackling impulses, the contours of their hunger, oceans surging within their bodies, exuberant and unrestrained. In that bed of passion, she forgot who they were, content for him just to be near her, and slept like a baby.

Saeed didn't experience quite the same feelings of elation. In the middle of autumn he spotted Salma. When she first disappeared into her aunt's house nearby, he had been unable to keep himself in check. Her image had been imprinted on the surface of his heart. His rising agitation was like a tempestuous sea. He drew a rose of life for himself adorned with the gold of predestined love. He was unable to continue to wait like that, in suspense. He was unaccustomed to confronting an onslaught like this galloping force. When he told his father he wanted to get engaged to her, he didn't understand Sitt al-Husn's shocked riposte, or why she bothered to comment at all. The next time they were alone together, he was in a dark mood, taut as a lute string.

In a voice energised by his newfound love, he told her, 'Tonight's the last night we're going to sleep together.'

She went along with him, even as the sound of creaking wood echoed deep down inside of her. She was deflated, crumpled like a scrap of paper. She became a single rose without a bouquet. When they were finished she withdrew into the corner, shivering in the cold that surrounded her.

In the morning signs of autumn were all over her: she was running a fever, she stopped eating, her joints creaked, she was unable to get up or move at all, refusing to speak to anyone. She stayed in bed until evening. She was shaking, and her fever wouldn't break.

She changed her clothes three times during the night. She was unable to get to sleep until after midnight, under the watch of Abu Saeed's bewilderment and sincere concern. Her sleep was punctuated by nightmares and states of panic. Her anxieties gnawed away at her in the mornings when she watched Saeed leave the house without having coffee or kissing her goodbye. He was uninterested in her minor seductions, desperate glances, the subtle signs of supplication or the erotic signals to which he had become so accustomed. He stopped noticing her altogether. She was nothing more than quarry he had spent a year of his life hunting.

When he came back in the afternoon, she was still in bed, too weak to stand even with her husband's dedicated assistance. She glared at him as he entered the room. He avoided looking her in the eye, sticking instead to a question about her health.

Her condition didn't last long. Several days later she got out of bed, nursing her wounds in an icy silence. This caused more satisfaction than fear for Saeed, who spent the ensuing days thinking mostly about Salma. This spared him any sense of bitterness and shame towards Sitt al-Husn. He was certain that whatever lingering connection they still had to one another would soon pass. Yet now, here she was in the spirit of rekindled affection. Although it was only from her side, those feelings washed over him even as he thought fondly about Salma, whose warm beauty had always left him awestruck.

What he failed to realise was that Sitt al-Husn's apparent retreat was only the calm in the eye of a hurricane.

She didn't go with them to propose to Salma. When they came back, she realised that an agreement had been made. Her vehement reaction – leaping up to embrace Saeed and kiss him on the cheek – stunned them both.

The stench of the dead leaked out of her mouth. Her body fluttered like a leaf. The two men exchanged a meaningless glance. Saeed couldn't understand what she was up to, feeling a mixture of disgust, panic and surprise from the foul stench in her mouth, her idiotic behaviour and ambivalent response. Still, when he retreated to bed without switching on the lamp, he was filled with relief at having rid himself of the illicit relationship with his father's wife that weighed on his conscience. As far as he was concerned, their separation was permanent. But Sitt al-Husn spent the entire night tossing and turning, convinced she was entering the twilight of her life. There was no going back, no way around the fact that their relationship was finished. But the only lesson Saeed was going to learn from it would be the one she intended for him. If she was good at waiting, she was even better at revenge. And so, when they brought Salma's nightshirt to Sitt al-Husn on their wedding night and she saw the bunch of cherries hanging on a thin thread of blood, she burned with the fever of hatred, with enmity in her heart, borne of the hours of screeching she had to endure while the marriage was being consummated.

She threw it down in disgust and exclaimed, 'Open your eyes! This wouldn't be enough for a chicken!'

Those words were spoken far away in time, but the poisoned shards of their prophecy continue to resonate today. From that moment, she was certain she had been sentenced to death by the woman who was going to sleep in her beloved's bed.

Confident in his own masculinity, Saeed thought of what Sitt al-Husn had said and Salma's elderly aunt's hollering as a test. He was bewildered by the sense of defeat. It certainly hadn't been his best performance, having finished in just five minutes. He went back to see Salma a second time. She had dressed. He prevented her from going to sleep, then he carried out his mission once again, deflecting her entreaties and her pleas.

The bleeding didn't stop until very late that night. The women gathered around Salma. She was flat on her back, her thighs clamped shut, as the blood spread.

Sitt al-Husn slept well, satiated by the feeling of victory, the victory of one who takes revenge after waiting patiently for several days.

☾

But now, this morning, she realised just how badly she had miscalculated the timing. Salma had run away and she was never coming back. Nobody would ever forgive Sitt al-Husn for what she had done. Everything she had planned, from her wedding night right to this very moment, seemed like mere child's play. She might be the only loser, and her loss would be substantial. After all, it is impossible to ask a dead woman about stolen gold.

She went out into the courtyard. A mountain of anxiety weighed upon her heart. What she missed most after Salma was the gold. She spun around in circles aimlessly. She blamed herself for what was happening all around her. She was set on confessing to her mistakes. She felt she had made a lot of missteps on her path towards revenge against Salma. Perhaps the most dangerous of all was her certainty that, even after all those months of bitter suffering, Salma had had no idea about the deception hiding behind Sitt al-Husn's convincing pretence of good intentions towards her.

It wasn't possible to turn back time. Everything was finished, over and done with. What made her fear even worse was this nagging obligation to face up to the catastrophe on her own, as if what happened had been permanently hitched to the wagon of her life.

Still under the sway of disordered thoughts, Sitt al-Husn found herself knocking on her neighbour Umm Mut'ib's door. The old widow was awake. When she opened the door in greeting, her corpulent body filled the entire passageway. Her enormous breasts spilled out of her collar; on either side of her face, the hennaed, greyish hair sticking out of her torn white scarf looked like horsehair. Sitt al-Husn collapsed into the old woman's arms, in tears, before telling her about the plague that had ravaged the garden of her life.

The old woman hesitated before responding and watched the woman weeping beside her as she chewed on a strand of hair she had started to braid.

All of a sudden, right before her eyes, Sitt al-Husn lost the special quality she had successfully woven into her personality over the two years since she had got married. Now there was nothing interesting about her. An ordinary woman no different from the market women for whom nothing in the world mattered besides their own fates. Her familiar attitude, the glamour of her perfumed clothing and all the artificial charms that she used to show off in front of everyone, making her seem like a woman of the world, all of it just dissipated.

News of Salma's flight didn't surprise Umm Mut'ib, but she was taken aback by the lightning bolt of hatred directed towards Sitt al-Husn that suddenly crashed through her heart. She couldn't get a single kind word out of her mouth. Despite her bitterness she managed to retain her composure, readjust her bright white headscarf and help Sitt al-Husn up.

'Come on,' she said.

'I'm feel like I'm going to faint,' Sitt al-Husn replied with a strange kind of frailty.

'All right, come on. Let's get you back to your house.'

Sitt al-Husn obeyed her brusque command, as rough as a boulder. The old woman let her anger loose, firing it like a stinging arrow.

Responding to the order, Sitt al-Husn tried to empty her voice of any shame or sorrow that had taken root in her body, saying 'Yes, ma'am', but she didn't have the strength, and her voice came out tense and muted instead. She got up with Umm Mut'ib's help, like a corpse animated by a feverish frenzy, as ghostly voices came and went and strange human forms appeared in the faint light of the foggy morning.

Back home all by herself, she felt like she was going crazy. The fog grew increasingly dense. Suddenly she found herself mulling over her present life, its hopeless emptiness. Time's betrayals had swallowed up all its vigour and beauty. The one thing she had stashed away as a defence against backstabbing and defamation – the gold – was gone, and it might never be found.

A little while later Umm Mut'ib did come back, though. She had run off to tell her brother Sayyah what had happened. The big man chewed on his moustache as he listened to her, and she noticed his hands were trembling. Once or twice he wiped the sweat from his brow then said, agitated, 'And what were you going to do?' He told her he wasn't going to be fooled by her veil of innocence. He didn't believe that Salma could get away from her aunt just like that, and he scolded her blisteringly. He was trying to suppress the anger that had, for some reason, taken him over, and his widowed sister, Abu Saeed's nearby neighbour, was an easy target.

His position disappointed Umm Mut'ib, who didn't know how to behave. When she returned home, the only difference was that her feelings of bitterness and lack of sympathy towards Sitt al-Husn's misfortune had gone away. She had allowed the winds of hate to blow. She couldn't hide it even though her only job now was to keep Sitt al-Husn quiet. She believed that the young people in the family would manage to bring Salma home by that afternoon. Her brother promised her as much, convincing her with his swift and savage anger.

It was a difficult task. She resented being obliged to pay her respects to a woman she had come to despise more than anyone in the whole world. In order to ensure her silence, she would have to flatter her, to seduce her with all manner of sympathy.

'Go ahead and cry,' she told her, 'just don't tell anyone.' Briefly listening to the flutter of her heart, she said, 'When they bring her back, I'll cut off her hand and get you back your gold.'

That wasn't what she had wanted to say. She had intended to offer a few words of condolence that might help Sitt al-Husn pull herself together. What had driven her to utter such a horrible curse instead? She struggled to cover up the single teardrop that slid down the philtrum leading to her lips.

Sitt al-Husn didn't notice.

The old woman's face appeared crushed by a deep sadness as she begged, 'Please forgive us, Sitt al-Husn.' It was a strange entreaty from a woman as superstitious as Umm Mut'ib. The compliment the old woman wished to pay, which she came out with almost without thinking at all, was just the beginning of the scandal.

'I always knew she was a whore, but I never said a word,' Sitt al-Husn said. 'I kept my mouth shut.'

Umm Mut'ib couldn't believe that what she heard referred to her missing niece. She knew all about Sitt al-Husn's relationship with Saeed, and she had been prepared to remain silent about it forever if Sitt al-Husn hadn't said that. She had had a special relationship with her niece. The widow had refused to give up her three-room house that abutted a small field in which she tended a variety of plants and flowers after her husband died. When Salma moved in next door, she became a friend who was able to crack through the strange family saga that encircled her. The two of them were members of the Zeeb clan amid a sea of Kharsans. That had been enough for her over the course of the past year. A curtain of forgetfulness fell on her years of humiliation. Every morning she called Salma. Then she started calling her before sunrise or after a pleasant trip. They would always drink maté together, occasionally breaking that tradition with a few cups of coffee. It was rare for either one of them to miss their appointment. Once in a while, in order to keep things fresh, they would invite other women over in the morning to chat over maté and coffee, rotating their list of invitees.

But now she knew that she was going to stand up to her brother's authority. She felt disappointed, ridiculous, like there was no force on earth greater than her desire to drag Sitt al-Husn through the mud or throw her from the highest peak.

'Listen,' she threatened, 'if you ever say something like that again in front of me, I'll strangle you.' To make sure that her message got through, she repeated herself. 'D'you hear me? I'll strangle you, even on a moonlit night!'

Sitt al-Husn cried out. At first her body was wracked with cold. In that same moment she felt as though she had been alone from the moment she was born. As the old woman hoisted up her enormous bovine body, she was certain that she truly would strangle her. Nobody could have convinced her otherwise. Umm Mut'ib's face furrowed with hatred, her eyes radiating murderous rage.

The old woman stared into that gaping mouth and those terrified eyes, covered them with her heavy palms and told her, 'Don't say another word.'

When Sitt al-Husn's dilated eyes finally returned to normal, Umm Mut'ib hissed like an asp, muting her spite.

'Will you shut up?'

Sitt al-Husn nodded.

The old woman thanked her without gratitude and left.

Sitt al-Husn cried out. She remained there, frozen, desiccated, on the edge of her seat, wide-eyed, transfixed for a few moments by eerie shadows that resembled enormous monsters. Suddenly she wailed, filling up that sorrowful morning, destroying the wisdom of old women, the virtues of silence and the knots of family protection.

She no longer had the strength to go back inside. The screaming had immobilised her, left her powerless right outside her own front door. She realised that her attempts to keep everything that had happened a secret were all in vain. In that protracted screaming there was an unmistakable omen, because there is nothing quite like women's howling to summon the angel of death.

Umm Mut'ib recalled that she had been surrounded by wailing since the night before. Umm Qasim's daughter-in-law wailed as they rushed her and her son, burning up with a milk allergy, to the hospital. Umm Nayef wailed when she heard the news of her nephew's death. And Naseeba wailed when they engaged her to Yahya Ibn Nawwaf.

Umm Mut'ib passed out briefly once she was inside the house. Her head crashed into the frame of the low kitchen door, and when she came to the neighbourhood was buzzing with the faint voices of men, women and children. She started crying over Salma, now certain that she was dead. She considered Sitt al-Husn entirely responsible for her death. The bewildering question gnawing away at her, making her heart burn hot, was what could have caused Sitt al-Husn to fill the world with her screams.

It never occurred to Umm Mut'ib that Sitt al-Husn might have been afflicted with a sudden paralysis that left her unable to move. The people who came to her aid found her sitting where Umm Mut'ib had left her, reeking from the stench of urine after wetting herself out of fear.

Umm Mut'ib knew quite a bit about this kind of love that she had unequivocally sensed from the start. She had seen the furtive sparks shooting back and forth between

Salma and Abd al-Kareem's enchanted eyes. She had no stake in the matter of their love, no role to play, but still she breached the fortress of secrecy that those two lovers had so carefully constructed. She knew the path; one day she, too, had trodden along it all the way to Assaf Kharsan.

Contrary to what might be expected of a sixty-year-old woman, Umm Mut'ib hadn't stood in the way of their love. She never quite understood why her heart fluttered when she first became aware of it. Sin had nothing to do with it, and yet it was strange for her not to consider it a sin. But the thought simply never occurred to her. Her heart tensed. She had difficulty breathing. She felt like she was suffocating. When she finally got to bed, her sleep was troubled and filled with anxiety.

The tightness had let up by morning, replaced with a profound sense of pessimism and unhappiness. Her heart never misled her. She was frustrated because she couldn't make sense of her intuition this time. Later, in a moment of despair, she told Fatima that she, too, was implicated in Salma's death. 'I should have warned her.'

At Abu Saeed's house they gave Sitt al-Husn camomile tea with dried mint leaves to drink. Umm Qasim came over to recite the *Mithaq al-Nisa'* in its entirety, followed by some calming spells. Once she had been stabilised, the three women hurriedly kicked everyone else out, shut the door and changed her wet clothes, dumbfounded by the tremendous swelling all over her corpulent body. They were upset that Salma had run away, but their pity came to an end as soon as they heard about the gold's disappearance. Nevertheless, they upheld their duty to take care of this woman whose legs had been paralysed by her misfortune. When Umm Qasim got up to say goodbye, they expressed their gratitude to her. The verses from the *Kitab al-Hikma* that she recited had succeeded in bringing some calm to Sitt al-Husn's troubled soul. But they failed to notice that the spell hadn't done anything for her raw throat, which started producing rasping noises occasionally that were clearly quite painful and caused her to moan the whole morning.

Afterwards her throat became infected, and the infection turned into bronchitis. It became chronic, leaving her with a constant painful scratchiness in her throat and a perpetual thirst. Creeping paralysis caused her to lose her mind. She would fly off the handle when those mercilessly sarcastic jokes were told at her expense. They all thought this paralysis – from which she later recovered – was caused by the disappearance of her gold. But that wasn't it. It was the incomparable fear she felt when she realised that Umm Mut'ib really might throttle her. That feeling would plague her for the rest of her life. She never got her gold back. Salma proudly denied being so debauched as to behave like a common thief.

Even after Umm Mut'ib died, moonless nights never ceased to terrify Sitt al-Husn. The ritual of panic had become a part of life that she couldn't live without. She turned inwards. The cold dryness of her body kept her frozen, and the terror that emanated from her crushed soul stung her face.

She wasn't fooled by the atmosphere of tenderness that the women created all around her. They were making fun of her. Until the car came to take her to Suwayda, the hours seemed long, endless. The day had been ruined. The dew lifted quickly, and the July sun shone fiercely.

4

The Guardian

When the news of Salma's death reached him, Sayyah Zeeb bowed his head momentarily. He examined the ground with his thick cane, closed his eyes and drifted off into a sea of memories. It all seemed like a dream to the old man, as if he were sleeping.

Lifting his head, it was a great effort for him to summon the strength to command in a calm voice, 'Bury her.'

For five years the women had held on to the shroud in which they would wrap her body. They had bought it from a travelling salesman and had set it aside for her future death. And now they thought back on this with a clear conscience.

They only needed a small section of the cloth. Hunger and extended captivity in the storehouse had whittled her body down to skin and bones. She looked as though she had shrunk, lost so much weight that she seemed to be fading away. The old women wept as they washed her body, crying as if it were the first time they had ever seen a dead person in their miserable and empty lives. When they brought Umm Mut'ib over, she couldn't understand what could make her sisters, whom she would hate for as long as there was any life left in them, cry that way. Was it the dead girl? Or were they crying over the fleeting days they had spent in her company?

She kissed Salma and said, with a tenderness that spilled out from the crevices of her tender heart, 'Go to sleep.' Then, stroking her face and forehead, she whispered, 'Farewell.' Standing up, she cast one last hateful glance at the old women and left the room, shaking as she wept.

Jamil Zeeb looked despondent when he came by, struggling under the weight of a heavy burden. He hadn't forgotten about the unparalleled solitude of this dead girl underneath the white shroud, the same one who had spat in his face when they first brought her back a month ago. But the horror of her death overpowered his humiliation and resentment, replaced now by a strange, troubled feeling, a mixture of pity and regret, a sense of just how absurd the world could be.

As he approached Salma's corpse in order to lift the thin sheet from her face, his body responded automatically. He imagined her ghost suddenly taking flight right there in front of him, alive, coursing with blood. Over the past month he had forgotten what she looked like. She hadn't been around any longer. She had been dead to him ever since Sayyah Zeeb ordered that she be locked up in the horse shed. Now it was as if she were dying for a second time.

Jamil thought about human weakness and disappointment as he stared at her emaciated body under that flowing shroud and lamented, 'She's come back to us as a little girl.'

Contrary to proper decorum, they didn't send out death notices. And Sayyah Zeeb forbade the old women from weeping in public. Then he sent one of his daughters-in-law to go to see Umm Mut'ib and order her to keep quiet; his daughter-in-law didn't pass on the message explicitly but made it plain that Sayyah knew all about his sister's discretion – which she maintained – concerning the Zeeb family's reputation. She couldn't just shake off the family's honour the way she might take off a robe. The horror belonged to all of them.

Umm Mut'ib was so distraught that she cut her finger peeling potatoes. She knew full well that Sayyah would be willing to do anything to protect his family from scandal. The Zeebs didn't matter to her, though. She detested their shameless conspiracies and dirty wars, the machismo they paraded so loudly throughout the village. The more she thought about how this whole mess was because of poor little Salma and her lover, the more she wished for her own death.

She knew this was a sign of weakness. Inside her there was a vast, empty feeling with a deep-down tangle of wishes set aside for Salma's wellbeing. Unable to offer her any real assistance, Umm Mut'ib had done as much as she could. Conspiring on the side of love that hasn't been arranged properly is a sure path to death. Whatever hope she may have had stemmed from her belief in miracles and fate.

But no miracle ever came to pass.

Umm Mut'ib acquiesced to her brother's command and to fate's decree. While she didn't mention Salma's name to anyone, she never stopped thinking about her. Salma even started to appear in her dreams in the guise of a rose.

The old women similarly obeyed their brother's orders. They picked up Salma's corpse and carried it to the storeroom, placed it on top of two thick woollen mattresses and covered it with a wedding sheet. Then they went back to their room, sat down outside the door and stared at the sun, waiting for it to set.

They all knew their brother wouldn't allow the dead girl to be buried until night had fallen. They were careful not to stoke his anger by asking why or even enquiring about the burial preparations at all. The best they could hope for was that he would order them to bury Salma in the family poppy field. They were prepared to kiss his feet if it should come to that, despite the fact that he hadn't spoken to them in six years – not since they had given his second son Muhammad some money so that he could run away from his iron-fisted, controlling father and travel to Venezuela to seek his fortune. Muhammad hadn't sent his father a single letter since he left, which further concretised their hatred and the poisonous atmosphere between him and his sisters. Those old women weren't hurt when Sayyah forbade all contact between Muhammad and his sisters, nor were they too concerned about their dispute with him, but a state of panic gripped them every day since hearing from some returning travellers that Muhammad had vanished without a trace.

They had doted on him ever since he was a little boy.

His playfulness and cheekily childlike nature inspired a strange kind of motherliness in them that they had never felt before. What would he think of them if he ever found out that Salma had died on their watch? Later, the question would only intensify their pain, forever dangling over their heads. They dutifully submitted to the desolate emptiness of a lonely desert where he had left them to rot among crumbling ruins.

Sayyah Zeeb calmed down. The thirst for vengeance that had come over him after hearing about Salma's death had been quenched. Everything had been going well up until that point. The war he anticipated with Umm Mut'ib never broke out. And he played it cool when the *mukhtar* and a bunch of his men paid him a visit. He managed to maintain his easy-going demeanour and high spirits the entire time, although he couldn't keep it up once the men had gone. As he crossed the veranda between the guesthouse and the main house, there, among the scattered scraps of hay on the threshing floor, he spotted his only daughter Naseeba, the last of his many offspring still living at home. After hearing of Salma's death Naseeba sat amid a pile of furniture she had moved outside so she could clean the house. Umm Mut'ib had broken the news to her as she was coming back from the old women's house next door. She dressed all in black that day, contemplating her own destiny, and sat down to cry.

This was a real dilemma. Her father was more surprised by her black clothes than the sight of her tears. He didn't have the strength to behave the way he should; he felt poorly equipped, in need of rebalancing. A sense of loss spread inside of him, the loss of something he could never replace. His face was the colour of mud, and he struggled to keep himself from collapsing. Standing face to face with his tearful daughter, he held his breath and turned around, careful not to let her see his weakness. Deep down inside he wanted her to confront him, as he was certain that talking about it with her would lift the burden from his shoulders at this sickening moment. But she didn't. She just dried her tears, stood up with her head held high and pretended to be busy washing clothes. She was trembling, wishing she had the strength to say something, stand up straight in front of her powerful father, address him with any of the words that might come tumbling down from the mountain of anguish inside of her. In the end she did nothing.

Sayyah Zeeb lurked like a wolf. He knew well that his daughter didn't have the courage to confront him or challenge him or even talk to him about what was happening. Although it was the natural consequence of the past twenty years, now it bothered him somehow.

He once took pleasure in that automatic acquiescence, the obedience laced with respect and reverence that he received from siblings and relatives alike. But that had worn off, the whole thing now seeming altogether banal. Self-confidence had flowed from him like some kind of cosmic force ever since fate helped him to defeat Hamad Zeeb. Remembering his uncle, who had died from a sudden heart attack, he was struck by how much he turned out to be just like him, a man whose heart had been extinguished, doused by feminine affection. His struggle with

Hamad could be traced back to when he was still a little boy. Hamad's arrogance used to infuriate him, but deeply rooted family traditions prevented anyone from challenging the status of the elder, no matter what. In this conflict with his uncle, Sayyah could see nothing but failure ahead of him; he had become increasingly aware of what this defiant stance was likely to mean amid the conflicts between the Shaabiyya clan and the Tarshans. Sayyah's decisions were fuelled by his optimistic hopes and dreams of achieving the stature of the mountain's greatest *zu'ama'*, realising that siding with the Tarshans was the only way to guarantee that. But Hamad refused to go along with him. Their conversation was frosty, without any flare-ups, but curt, and neither one of them was going to back down. Sayyah mused that Hamad was like a soft yet stubborn donkey. He never had a chance to change his mind about this because Hamad passed away while Sayyah was off fighting in the Arab Liberation Army. When he returned from the front he discovered that Hamad's sudden death had left a mark like a scorched sapling on his family's morale; they would forever mourn the fruit it might have produced. He never dared to share his opinion with anyone. This would have only added further insult to the series of defeats he had already experienced. The War of 1948 would continue to put his manhood in question, the way he imagined it did to the manhood of all those fighters who had been with him the day they were forced to evacuate Shefa-'Amr.

When he returned home, he believed he would be content to spend the rest of his days as *za'im* of the Zeeb family. He kept secret his interest in the fate of the local quarrels and battles that he had been involved in here and there, informing everyone, as they draped him in the black robe of leadership, that he didn't want any dissension within the family. Decisions were his to make alone, and there was no need for him to say anything more.

But later it dawned on him that he didn't even have to say that. Life was no longer concerned about the fate of a single family, lost in the labyrinth of misfortunes that had beset the country, amid the growing power and repression of the regime. Sayyah no longer held much sway as a *za'im* beyond the sparkling nostalgia for a bygone age and the hearth of memories he kept afire. The fate of his family was slipping through his fingers like water: the famines of the fifties, exile and migration, prophesied news of an impending apocalypse. All of this disoriented him, especially as he was unable to shake off those fantasies of authority that he had concocted from his longstanding thirst for power.

Nevertheless, those returning from abroad would bring him gifts: a Kuwaiti-style embroidered shawl; a black *jubba* from the Hamidiyeh souk in Damascus; a *kufiyah* and matching cord; tailored long-sleeved robes; and a Browning 14-mm handgun, which he kept without a permit. Right up to the hour of his death, though, he never once threatened to shoot anyone. That would have run against his principles as *za'im* of the family, although it wouldn't upset him if somebody else carried out a revenge killing or even killed him to protect their own honour. He couldn't deny the fact that the handgun he kept carefully stashed behind one of the cushions energised him with beams of confidence, comfort and security.

But he didn't brag about it. Time delayed his dreams from coming true. All his plans sank into the muddy bogs that covered the fields of his life. He sold all the land he had inherited from his father. And, later, after Sayyah died, Saleem Nakadi turned up and shoved bills of sale amounting to ten thousand lira in his children's faces.

In the tumultuous days of his past, the fact that the traditional power of the *zu'ama* was no longer ensured didn't weaken his authority. It only prevented him from consolidating it any further. The family that seemed to have forgotten all about Sayyah Zeeb woke one day to discover that he had been thrown in jail, charged with belonging to a political party that was hostile to the regime. That was in 1959, during the heyday of spies and informers, when the regime considered being an informer to be definitive proof of treason.

Sayyah denied just about everything, despite the many varieties of torture he endured, but he never denied the fact that he had once hosted party members in his home – for reasons of hospitality and nothing more, as he insisted. Still, he sat in jail for eight months.

When he got out, he expected to face humiliation, but there was an even greater surprise waiting for him: the family had prepared a feast to celebrate his return. Dozens of people fired into the air out of joy, defying the orders and terrorism of the regime, which did nothing in retaliation. It was like a miracle: whether it was through him or simply because of him, everyone's floodgates of memory had burst open, illuminating and radiant, in a way that made up for Sayyah's feelings of defeat over the lost years of national discontent since 1948.

He had become a hero, unfortunately. He was stunned by the welcome, confounded by the ordinary feelings and humdrum emotion that accompanied such a celebration, which he thought could be attributed to the thanklessness of being a *za'im* at a time when the regime could install anyone they wished in that position. That night he was made even more miserable when his wife refused to sleep in the same bed with him because she had her period. Her condition was more powerful than his burning desire to sleep with her, and he had no choice but to give in.

And so, because of all that, he started to become pessimistic.

They made up a bed for him in the guesthouse, as was the custom, and he stayed awake for more than an hour, smoking and watching the fire flicker in the lantern as it climbed towards the neck of the glass. Feeling sleepy, he got up and blew it out with one strong puff. The very next moment the door opened, and a delicate, trembling apparition slipped inside. He didn't have time even to figure out what was going on before a panting woman crashed on to his lap, reeking of sex, soaked with dew. As she buried her head in his chest and smothered him with kisses, she seemed to be radiating lust.

He didn't need any encouragement. As gentle as a bird he moved her slightly, gazing at her face between his hands, and whispered with obvious delight, 'Linda? Hold on…' Like a cat he pounced for the door, locking it deftly.

When he turned around to find her getting undressed in the moonlight, he happily did the same.

When he was ready, she scolded him. 'You idiot! Ten years I've been waiting, but you never came to see me, not once!'

He squeezed her waist.

Moaning and gesturing at his crotch, she said, 'Don't worry about it. This is going to make up for everything.'

He couldn't see her clearly. In the days that followed, what went on between them that night seemed more like a hazy dream, translucent and gelatinous. But he would never forget the heat of her rosy flesh, fiery like a cauldron.

The memory recurred every day, for days after they said goodbye to one another. He thought long and hard about how she had behaved. What was even more confusing was the fact that he had barely noticed her heaving body before, despite the fact that they were separated by nothing more than a slapdash wall made out of piled-up furniture. He was thrilled that she had made the first move, believing that her coming to see him was one of the great rewards for his leadership and incarceration. From that moment on he spared her no expense, allowing her to benefit from her husband Qasim being away in Lebanon.

Linda ignited an inferno of licentiousness in him. In spite of his advanced age her body couldn't fully satisfy him. She was the fire that melted the seal of his stagnation, opening him up to a universe of sex that would only come to a close when he died, at seventy, from a bite by a rabid dog.

The next woman was Umm Samer. It was easy enough

to get to her, as she was the only one who would sleep with men for money. Having been denied sex for many years, he went to see her in a near stupor. Her husband received him warmly. Finally, Sayyah Zeeb had come to visit the two of them. Abu Samer believed that the blessing of this visit outweighed the gains of merely speaking with the head of the Zeeb family, as they would extend to them the protective wing of one of the most important village families and the power of its bravest men.

Sayyah never made as much profit as he did that night. He said he had come to visit the two of them because he knew Abu Samer would be there. Abu Samer didn't hold back his expressions of happiness and hospitality.

Sayyah hadn't even caught his breath yet when Umm Samer walked in, her ample chest held high, singing the praises of her night-time visitor. Her scorching feminine beauty dazzled him. That unexpected power and the violence of his desire led him to join the ranks of her lovers. He spent a few moments musing about how stupid it had been for him to ignore the insinuating gestures that Husayn Muzeed and Farhan Hassan had made in the past when suggesting he should go to visit her.

Umm Samer understood the secret of his visit. As they talked, she saw it in his eyes, his movements and his racing thoughts, convinced that, from this night on, luck was going to smile on her. She wasn't afraid of anyone. She hadn't opened a brothel after all. Her husband – as harmless as a fly – was of no concern to her. She didn't care whether or not he knew what she was up to.

But neither Sayyah nor those who visited Umm Samer

to sleep with her were ever totally sure what the arrangement was. Abu Samer was a night watchman in Suwayda who came home to sleep in his own bed only one night a week. He might say that some men had defiled his wife, but he never talked to her about it, too terrified of her fury and the savage strength of her body. He kept silent. He swallowed this existence, bite after bite, until he got used to it.

As far as she was concerned, the power of the visit had to with Sayyah himself. He was the only man who could give her goose pimples, but she never thought he would ever dare to visit her. She made do with some peasants and the notables of two lesser local families, carefully selected from among the virile men of the village; her inerrant instinct in these matters had her convinced that one of them would be able to make love to her all night long.

The only man with whom she violated her own habits was Abd al-Kareem. She was pained by his weakness and his frailty, believing that she could empower him just by being with him, that she could repair his troubled soul and his shattered body.

Two nights later Sayyah came to see Umm Samer at the hour she had specified. After locking the door on her two sleeping children, she was ready to get going, to receive him in her bedroom.

The room was bathed in the light of a lantern hanging near a large mirror in a beech-wood frame engraved with roses and leaves. Everything was new: the curtains, the sewing-machine cover, the tablecloth, the ocean-coloured carpet and the tree-print bedspread.

With a grin on his face he asked, 'Do you really need such a trap?'

She applauded his wit and replied, 'This guest room is reserved for only the finest men!'

The idea astonished him, and without thinking he whispered, 'Lock the door and get over here next to me.'

Shaking her head, she smiled as she assured him, 'Don't you worry. If another man comes into the room while you're here, I'll cut his balls off!'

He never let go of Umm Samer, although he wasn't about to give up Linda without a fight, this despite the fact that he slept with a lot of women in the village and visited houses of prostitution in Damascus, Aleppo and Lebanon. He always came back to Linda, his original point of departure, who responded to his call right away. He paid no mind to the days ahead. Linda encouraged him when, totally naked, she swore she would remain his property until death did them part. Their relationship had been interrupted by long periods of separation. But each and every time they got back together Sayyah was affected by a kind of desire that drove him mad.

Although his wife's intuition warned her that something was amiss, she kept silent when he threatened to divorce her. She would have had to muster a great deal of energy just to tell him how she felt; it took a comparable amount of effort to swallow this bitter pill. Sayyah considered himself free of any obligation to her. He took her silence as tacit agreement to his privileges as a man and as the *za'im* of the Zeeb family.

Linda kept her promise until he sold off all his land

and no longer had anything left to offer. She continued to visit him when she could, but that became less frequent. Her children had grown up, and she started to fear them. The last time he could remember was the night before her husband, Qasim, came back from Lebanon.

'Wish me a fond farewell,' she told Sayyah.

He slept with her twice. The next day she jokingly told him about how Qasim had remarked that her vagina seemed wider than it used to be.

Sayyah had no regrets. He never fully believed his immature sense that Linda was the reason for his downfall. He had sold off all his land in order to make himself happy. That was good enough; he didn't think it had been a mistake. Whenever necessary, he went to work with the contractor Hasan Rayyes, who offered him honest work that preserved whatever vestiges of dignity he still had left.

His brother Salman was already dead from throat cancer. The illness lasted only a few months. Sayyah now found himself responsible for his brother's wife and their daughter Salma. But his sister-in-law chose her own path: she married Sayil Hamad and moved to the Jazeera region in the north-east, leaving her eight-year old daughter behind in the charge of her uncle.

Sayil warned Sayyah's wife, Umm Muneer, not to get too close to Salma. She responded by raising the subject of the maternal obligations of Salma's mother, who in turn retorted that she wasn't going to dig herself an early grave. Life was too short, she said.

When Sayyah declared that widows in the Zeeb family

don't remarry, his sister-in-law scoffed. 'Your women are like serpents. Smooth and unclean!'

She was cut off from the family. Sayyah wouldn't hesitate to badmouth his wayward sister-in-law, especially when he learned that she had run off with half the furniture his brother left behind. But he didn't actually do anything that would get in the way of her marriage. Given her headstrong response, he was convinced that bringing her daughter home to ensnare her in the web of family would be a thousand times easier than keeping both eyes open in order to watch over a young widow who didn't want to be constrained.

Much later, after Salma's death, he thought he had made a mistake, because her mother never showed up in the village. Some of the party functionaries who came back from Hassakeh told him that she learned of her daughter's death sixth months after Salma had already been laid in the ground, but she kept her mouth shut because she wasn't happy at the idea of having to tell her other children about the scandalous fate of their older sister.

It was like a game. On more than one occasion he thought about sending someone to threaten her so that she'd keep her mouth shut. The plan emerged from his desire to erect some kind of barrier, whether imaginary or real, in the face of anyone who would try to ferret out his tortured soul by brandishing the spectre of that murdered girl. He was in dangerous territory, threatened by worldly scandal and divine retribution. He inhabited the bloody wound that was his decision, the scar of an anxious and dishevelled mind. Then his sister-in-law's messenger came to ferry him to safety. She eventually accepted Salma's death as if she were the perpetrator. At least, that was his understanding.

Salma's presence in the house alongside his daughter Naseeba had restored his optimism. All his sons had abandoned him early on: Muneer moved far away after getting married; Fu'ad chose military service after he flunked out of school; Hayil became an alcoholic very young – he was destroyed by it, dissolved into oblivion; after Muhammad emigrated to Venezuela there was no further contact with him.

Sayyah's dreams of going abroad and making the family proud were dashed. One day, in his first attempt to get to know the two of them better, he invited them to go to Suwayda with him in order to stock up on supplies. The two girls didn't sleep the night before because travelling to Suwayda at that time was a rare honour for ten-year-old girls. They stayed up late planning out the next day's activities. Standard travel practice was well known: the bus wouldn't arrive before eight a.m., and even though it was no more than forty kilometres to Suwayda, they had heard accounts of a bumpy dirt road and a jalopy that would get them there but leave them feeling like weary immigrants.

The brown, dusty morning didn't diminish their excitement. They braided each other's hair and put on the nicest clothes they owned: tree-print dresses, socks as white as snow, black shoes with red embroidered flowers on the toes. Without making a fuss about it, Naseeba took off her belt when she noticed that Salma didn't have one. But they didn't have the nerve to find their travelling companion, thinking more than once that he must have already left and abandoned them there. When they finally heard his voice calling for them, they both started to cry.

The journey was thrilling for them. Nature was multi-layered. Golden fields stretched out and shimmered endlessly. The morning was alive with squawking birds and the aroma of fresh earth. The screeching metal of the bus was a fast-paced rhythm that dissolved into the jostling voices of the twenty passengers. A never-ending sequence of black telephone poles. They both fell into silence.

In Suwayda he bought them matching dresses, dolls whose eyes closed when they reclined, colourful silk ribbons, long, thin sweets and some novelty lizard eggs. When they had finished shopping, he asked the two girls if they were hungry, and they whispered, like shrinking violets, that they wanted falafel, so he bought two fresh sandwiches. They ate them while they waited for the bus driver, who was delayed, taking pleasure in tormenting all the other envious girls as they savoured the pleasure of well-spiced food.

Sayyah Zeeb was no less satisfied. Twenty-five years on, as he lay on his deathbed, his body ravaged by feverish madness, this memory would come back to him as a kaleidoscopic vision of two girls in the flower of their youth, smiling against the backdrop of a sunflower stalk.

Years later, when they went to speak to Salma after she had been brought back from eloping with Abd al-Kareem, he still couldn't believe that the innocent girl who had never asked for anything more than a falafel sandwich in her entire life could be the very same woman who stood up to him and Jamil Zeeb.

He couldn't recall who had convinced whom to tell her about the decision but Sayyah felt betrayed after having shown Salma what he considered to be such kindly fatherliness. She took after him in following her wild bodily desires and sinful lust, the same pursuits that had brought him back to life after a period of hibernation. By running off with Abd al-Kareem, she severed the ties that people considered to be the most sacred. She had disappointed her family, besmirched their honour and dragged their names through the mud of scandal. After the police brought her home, their shame echoed around the entire mountain region. They had lost their good reputation. Their heads would hang in shame forever. What more lay in store for them?

Sayyah was horrified at the new woman she had become. He was accustomed to having girls and women panic whenever they encountered him. He could tell from the way their legs shook or the way their tongues froze in their mouths. His power was thunderous. He was puffed up by the sense of being in charge, even though his behaviour had created a rift between him and all the women around him, one that time could never bridge. His house was overflowing with women whose only concern was to attend to his family line. His marriage was stable. If an emotional storm were to sweep over him, it wouldn't rattle his solid foundation, although it might leave a lasting mark. If Umm Muneer kept silent for fear of the scandal that might come crashing down on her family, his relationship with Linda was a trespass for which she would never forgive him. While his sisters remained subservient to his tyranny, his relationship with them had been severed ever since Muhammad went away. The only woman who dared to challenge him was Umm Mut'ib, whom he disowned after she married Assaf Kharsan. The presence of those obedient women convinced him that God had bestowed tremendous blessings upon him. His wife relieved him of the duty to take care of their sons and daughters. The old folks pitched in as well. The isolation that was imposed upon them opened up a critical distance that nobody would ever be able to cross. But at the end of his life, even before that rabid dog bit him, he would lament the fact that he had lived like a mangy camel. He never dreamed that one day he would die bundled up in a carpet, tossed in a corner of the storehouse above the horse shed, suffocating, dying of thirst and shaking uncontrollably.

Salma was another woman altogether. On the day she ran off, Sayyah was preparing the animals to be slaughtered on the occasion of the village hosting Prince Salaam. After twenty-five years Sayyah's dream of becoming part of the élite leadership in the mountain region was finally coming true. Prince Salaam enjoyed the approval and support of the regime, having kept his hands clean since childhood in one of the most prominent families. He was the one who handed an entire cell of a banned political party over to the security services. Then he forced out the rank-and-file members of another party by putting pressure on their mothers and fathers through intimidation. From that point on he attempted to write himself into a history of generosity, every few months inviting important officials, ministers and high-ranking officers over for lavish banquets.

The fruits of his labour were clear. He was given the honorific title of 'Prince', in spite of the shame that had followed him ever since he had kidnapped his grandfather's wife and holed up with her in a Beirut hotel for fifteen days.

On the day Sayyah heard the news that Salma had run away, he wept, also swearing that she was a whore who would pay the price for his tears and for the violation of his honour. Death would be too good for her. He recommended locking Salma up in the horse shed, an idea the family supported. The crazy thought of killing her wasn't his, but it acquired a talismanic power once it was put out there nonetheless.

Despite the brutality of that response, and the foulness of retribution and murder, the proposal turned out to be acceptable to everyone who had assembled to discuss the matter, or so it seemed at the time. This prospect was something new to all of them, something that, as Hayil Masoud Zeeb put it, they would have no choice but to experience for themselves once they took that course of action.

Salma had become a different woman altogether. In her slit white skirt, her blouse perforated along the neckline with a jagged starched collar, the rays of sunlight shining down on her and her ponytail through the window that was crisscrossed with metal bars, she looked like a blossom, bright as a summer's day, gentle. Sayyah Zeeb was stirred up, fervidly energised to snuff out this budding rose.

Their conversation didn't last long. He told her that she had tarnished the Zeeb family honour, that their dignity had been compromised and that she truly deserved to die, although the police would never allow it. That was why the scandal had caused such alarm, he told her. Sayyah shuddered as he expressed his disappointment in her. He was crestfallen. He did not mince his words: she had to die. Nothing but death could erase the grotesque and humiliating memory from this world.

'She *deserves* to die,' Jamil interjected unexpectedly. Seeing the exhaustion written all over his uncle's face, he went on to tell Salma that they weren't going to let a young man from the Zeeb family be contaminated with her impure blood, and if any one of them spent even a minute in jail because of her it would be like an eternity. She was going to die there.

Salma didn't understand anything that was happening to her. Despite Jamil's venomous sermon and Sayyah's vicious comments about her imminent death, they never detailed just how it was going to happen.

Jamil's dry, wizened face stared back at her when she tried to stand up. Once she had sought refuge in him. Any time the spectre of being an orphan suddenly loomed over her, she found comfort in his prying eyes, which could also be filled with powerful affection. Whenever he talked to her about the memory of her father and all the time they had spent together, she was soothed by the warmth of his uncommon tenderness. But now he looked more like a wolf, wounded by disappointment, a stealthy killer.

She knew that her life was over. The ship of fate had to depart now that her safe harbour had been destroyed. She could detect the sour taste of death under her tongue.

She could never have anticipated this moment. She was stunned. She surrendered to her destiny without a word, just like that. How strange it all seemed. Then there was the canyon of despair that had been lurking between the hills of her happiness. She felt like a victim of treasonous destiny, of mistaken and unsettled scores. Just for an instant, though. She had no regrets. And why not? This ephemeral happiness had once been something so real she could reach out and touch it in the same way she touched stone and fruit and the red roses she loved so much, the happiness of two lunatics enjoying the bounty of life and sucking out its marrow. One could always respond to fate's betrayal, even as it drove human beings on towards the finish line.

She had to say something. Her fate was wrapped up with the figure of Jamil, Jamil the untrustworthy, dripping with spite, bubbling over with a deathly fever. She stepped towards him, gazed at his decrepit face and desiccated eyes, scrutinised the wrinkles crowding the small darkened space separating lips from forehead, inspected his shrunken frame as if he were a corpse brought low from the pinnacle of maturity. Her life force awakened, she spat in his face with all the strength she could muster.

He lunged at her, smacked her as hard as he could and shouted:

Die!
Die!
Die!

Nobody could say who first proposed the idea of killing her, and nobody mentioned what went on at that meeting until ten years after Salma's death, when Jamil Zeeb, finding a shard of broken glass in a piece of bread he was about to eat, bellowed instinctively, 'Are you trying to kill me the same way you did Salma?'

5

The Lovers

Their love began in the morning. The green Land Rover was creeping towards Suwayda. It was seven thirty. Sitting in the back seat, he surveyed the other passengers, then the winding road. He spotted two crescent-shaped eyes staring back at him through the convex rear-view mirror, as if they were keeping watch. He tried to ignore that brief encounter but found himself in thrall to an invisible desire to understand the situation. He slowly turned in his seat, taking in everything, all the passengers, until he arrived back at the mirror. Those eyes were still there, wide open and radiant. They had not turned away from him. Only the distance between the front and back seat separated them. The curvature of the mirror made her eyes appear to be floating in a wide-open sky, illuminated by a warm, powerful sun, speckled with rainclouds. He was nervous. What did she want? Was she really looking at him, or was this a fantasy projecting what he wanted to see? He thought for a moment that the vibration of the mirror was what made her eyes seem to be looking at him so intently. Or that in her uncomfortable spot right beside the driver she couldn't move or adjust her position. Should he look back at her? He was nervous about what was going to happen next, realising how potentially embarrassing it would be for him to respond, trembling the way he did whenever he was forced to confront something new. There was no way around this, though. He wasn't going to restrain himself this time. This potential enemy in wait for him wasn't hiding or backing down. Still, even if she really was looking at him and had the courage to stare at him like that inside a small vehicle crammed with passengers, it could only mean that she must be crazy.

He was brought out of his anxious reverie by the tremendous amount of energy he had to muster just to lift his gaze up to the mirror once again, to make contact with the eyes of a woman he would fall in love with in a way that was unlike his love for anyone else on the face of the earth. Those eyes were right there, waiting for him – deep spaces shaded with honey and shimmering light, twinkling like stars in the summertime, fragile and melancholy.

There was no power in the universe strong enough to prevent what happened a few minutes later. His heart nearly burst, blood rushed to his face, his scalp was on fire as warm sweat oozed, thick and sticky, all over his body: he loved the possessor of those reflecting eyes, now and forever.

It wasn't until much later that he learned who she was. He had heard her name mentioned before, caught some talk of her beauty. But he never imagined that such brightness could be stored in her eyes. They glowed with an invisible charge and cut straight to his heart, overwhelming him with love in an instant. She filled up his life, coating the cracks and gaping holes in his monotonous routine, blowing through him like winds of supercharged happiness. All his doubts and unresolved issues, dreams and fears of the unknown, were transformed into a kind of easy confidence, erasing the pages of years gone by while simultaneously sketching out a paradise of the days to come.

He didn't hesitate. He knew that two days later she would be going out to the harvest with her great-uncle, that at ten o'clock she would pass by Wadi Saeed on her way home. He saw her approaching. The sun poked through the gauzy June clouds. Several women followed behind her, more than fifty metres in the distance. He saw children riding a donkey, others guiding cattle that were lowing or dragging along the morning feed for the herd. As she got closer he saw a dusty sky-blue scarf wrapped around her head, held in place by a red sash. For a moment he considered not talking to her at all. That he had even thought this would stun him later, because if he had decided not to approach her, he would have dashed any hopes of being happy for eternity. He quickly abandoned this train of thought, noticing how extraordinary she looked in that otherwise everyday village scene.

Salma knew who he was. She cursed herself for breaking away from her friends at the harvest, arriving here ahead of them, realising that now she would have to say hello to him. As she contemplated the distance separating her from the other women, she realised there was no use in hanging back or waiting for them. She was even more distraught over the fact that she wouldn't have the chance to make herself presentable before the encounter. She pretended not to see him. She lowered her eyes to the ground. She ignored him altogether. She stumbled a few times along the bumpy country road, giggling at how curiously detached she felt. Once it seemed as though she was going to be able to slip by without having to say hello, she lifted her head, but there he was, right in front of her. Everything she had done to avoid him came to nothing. She fluttered like a butterfly.

Abd al-Kareem would later tell her that she had been on the brink of tears. She denied it by saying, 'I was just tired, worn out from the sun.'

They both went out of their way to behave with exaggerated civility. The whole situation turned melodramatic because of their invented characters. He asked her where she was coming from.

'Heaven,' she replied with a smile.

This response astonished him.

Sensing this, she tried to walk back her ironic tone. 'What about you?' she asked.

'We're a fine match,' he said, laughing. 'I come from earth!'

Neither one of them had anything more to say. They both wished the awkward encounter to come to an end. But his moribund emotions had been stirred. Abd al-Kareem hurriedly said goodbye, smitten with love that might smash through his calm demeanour at any moment.

He felt like an idiot when he recalled his inability to utter even a single word that might convey the feelings their encounter had inspired in him. He remembered all too well how he had to struggle against his dim-wittedness, his inadequate, tortoise-like thinking. He blamed himself for the lukewarm way in which she had greeted him. Those moments just after their encounter were maddening. How could two eyes assault another's heart with such force, with godly power? Later on, even after they began seeing each other regularly, he couldn't get used to her eyes, their unfiltered shimmering, their fire.

This disorientation unnerved Salma, too. Her anxiety grew because they couldn't share their secret with anyone. She felt acutely alone as well. Her husband had departed for Venezuela. Her family never visited. She was forced to live in a lonely house with a woman who hated her even more than everybody else did.

She retreated inwards, gnawing on whatever happiness she still had left but without much appetite. Because it represented a way to put an end to her isolation, she thought that giving up on her secret love carried more risk than reward. A married woman was expected not to fall in love. Unfortunately, there was not only one family but two hovering over her: the Zeebs and the Kharsans. The men in both families talked about little other than killing immoral women. That was reason enough to bury her secret deep down inside. But this never really dissuaded her fully. She floated along the gushing spring of love all the way out into the field of her life. She would steer discussion of both important issues and minor events towards the same topic: love. She saw no harm in that. She would go out to the harvest without complaining, carried along by her dreams, driven by her wish to run into Abd al-Kareem on the road or just to catch a distant glimpse of him out in the field.

Then, to her astonished delight, she was assigned the chore of hauling water to the house from the only well in the village square. Every trip would take her in front of his house. On one occasion she nearly confessed her feelings. But she simply kept on carrying the water jug back and forth on her shoulder well into the late afternoon, until all the jars and buckets and bottles in the house were full. Abd al-Kareem didn't appear that day. Seeing him once would have brought her to a halt. Just before the last trip, Sitt al-Husn stepped in to prevent her from going. Her eyes were filled with suspicious concern communicating a kind of guile that shook Salma out of her lovesick daze.

That evening she thought long and hard about telling her aunt what was going on, but after evaluating the situation she decided that it was better not to. That was her one false move in this romantic adventure. After a while the old woman Umm Mut'ib found out everything anyway. But she couldn't talk to her niece about what it all meant, or, that is, she didn't know exactly what to tell her. Salma's newfound passion made it hard for Umm Mut'ib to see things clearly. All she could do was continue feeding Salma well, making up for the insufficient meals she received at home. Salma would laugh at the old woman as she stuffed her face full of food, telling her, 'I'm going to get as fat as a cow!'

When his symptoms of love first started to appear, everyone who knew him became concerned about Abd al-Kareem. The signs were obvious: he became obsessed with his appearance; he stood in front of the mirror like an adolescent, combing his hair and slathering it with shiny brilliantine; every day he ironed one of the two pairs of trousers that he owned, laying the other out on the guest bed; he shaved despite the nicks his blunt razor left on his chin; he stayed out late.

When he first fell in love with her, he would sit out on the upper balcony, taking pleasure in gazing up at the stars in the June sky. But as his feelings grew, this was no longer enough for him. He started to go out every night after ten for walks, stalking the village streets around Salma's neighbourhood just to steal a glimpse of her bedroom window or her shadow if she happened to be awake, knowing full well that she was forced to go to bed early so that she could rise before dawn for the harvest.

But this didn't last long. One night he was paralysed with horror after he heard that Salem Abboud had killed himself inside the school after failing the graduation exam for the eighth time. He could imagine him there in the moonlight, scaling the wall, looping a rope over the steel girder that extended across the classroom ceiling. Abd al-Kareem was about to cry out to his vision of Salem, but a sudden movement shut him up: Salem slipped his head through the noose and plunged into the void. After this he stopped going out at night, even though a burning desire to do so convulsed his entire being. The only thing that made him feel better was sharing the secret with his friend Haleem Hammoud.

'That's the best news I've heard!' Haleem said with the

glow of someone who has discovered something rare. He squeezed his hand and then whispered, 'Now your path to her is wide open.' Haleem snickered momentarily then started to philosophise about the situation, droning on about his own experience with women.

There was nothing for it. Grape juice isn't the same as fresh fruit on the vine. He wasn't just looking for a fling. He had known that from the very first moment. And because Haleem wasn't actually the libertine he made himself out to be, his hyperbole and inflated ego meant that he was not to be trusted. Abd al-Kareem decided that he would spend the rest of that evening alone working out the best way to connect with Salma.

He decided to track her movements, to find out any news he could about the family she lived with, to come up with a workable way of finding his way to her. Several times he bumped right into her on the street. They would exchange pleasantries – one of them might ask the other how it was going – but it was impossible to talk about affairs of the heart. He was held back by vague feelings that she would stop him if he tried to move the conversation in a romantic direction. What if all of this came to nothing? The idea shredded him.

His sleuthing lasted almost two weeks. He used both disguise and deception to direct the gossip between his mother and those women who came to visit towards the subject of Salma. He tried to find out whatever he could from his sister and his friends. What he came up with was hardly enough to create a clear picture of the situation, and the patchy details sent him into a state of panic, especially on the day when he learned how nervous everyone was around Sitt al-Husn. He was certain that it was because of her powerful, domineering personality as much as her vulgarity and the poisonous relationship she had with her stepson, Saeed, that she didn't attempt to hide. Meanwhile, Abu Saeed left a colourless, unappealing impression. A subdued man, the years had leeched away any trace of masculinity in him that the villagers might be able to admire.

The portrait painted by what he heard about the Zeebs wasn't exactly complimentary either. They seemed like ghosts, distinguished by their antipathy and an uncon-cealed desire to rule over the village. He knew a few of their boys: Hammoud, Akram and Salman. But they didn't have any real power, and he dismissed them without a second thought. Someone showed him an image of Sayyah Zeeb, gigantic in front of a tall, impenetrable stone wall, surrounded by women and children from his family who flocked around his arrogance and bluster. He had detested this man ever since hearing the talk that had been cooked up in the village cauldrons, fatty and salty, seasoned with wild speculation and presumptuous-ness, most of which never came to pass. Still, the only photograph anyone seemed to have was this same one, which Abd al-Kareem had seen before. He watched as if his enemy were approaching, full of ferocity, touched by fire, drained of all colour. A black-and-white photograph without any sense of composition.

That was enough information for him; the door was shut as far as he was concerned, leaving open a window that looked out upon Salma's verdant fields. What he heard was enough to scotch any plans they might make. A single miscalculation could turn everything upside down.

He couldn't be sure who or what had convinced him of the idea. Was it an illusion or a trustworthy ally? He was sure that a woman like Salma could only have been forced into marrying as immoral a man as Saeed. A sad bird in a wicked hunter's cage. A rose sucked dry by insects that feed on the freshness of youth. Images of his miserable beloved were bathed in blood, coloured red with unhappiness and stripped bare, underexposed. He rang out the bells of scandal, which strengthened his resolve as he rallied to the idea of saving her from the thistles and the wolves. A redeemer who would deliver her from the debilitating weakness that afflicted her. In this way he would also be able to save his own soul from cowardice and uncertainty amid the climate of panic that had loomed over him ever since he heard the news of the Zeeb and the Kharsan families. Deep down inside he saw many things: nature suddenly empowering him with unconquerable strength; his embracing Salma without trepidation; their enemies cowering in fear.

In another dream he was high in the air, as if he had wings, journeying to a wondrous land with chestnut and carob trees. The vision inspired high hopes for his big decision, at which point Salma would be free and ready to marry him. In that dream the two of them were somehow able to meet, talking in the heat of a moonlit night – but she seemed ill, struck down with a kind of sadness more like starvation. He embraced her underneath a giant china tree, gnats and ants all around them, her body emitting miasmatic agony. As dawn broke she clung to him defiantly.

After he awoke he spent the whole day convinced they really had met. It was undeniable. He felt at peace, all his anxieties and fears had dissipated. That evening, though, he started to get nervous when he truly understood it had all been a dream. Now he had to beat back those terrible thoughts and his own addled mind.

It was madness.

He spent the next few days weighed down by feelings of confusion. He felt powerless and disappointed, caught in the closed loop of his searching. He was worn out by the monotonous routine of everyday life. He would be woken up at five a.m. by the sheep bleating in their pen, the stifling morning heat as they staggered forward like zombies, nestling their heads in the curves of their sisters' bodies, the one crazy ewe that always wandered off. The first rays of sunlight as they crept into his room. The early-morning screeching of his brother Salman's children, Salman who still couldn't leave the house after eight years of marriage. His sister Dalal's voice as she sang along to Fairuz, her tongue lashing out at him whenever he dared to reproach her. The mechanical tightening in his heart whenever his father complained about the poor harvest from the small plot of land they farmed, or about his perpetual inability to find a suitable caretaker for their home.

His morning cup of maté with the family no longer excited him. Boredom overpowered him whenever he tried to read. The gateways of his imagination were shut tight. His faculties were obstructed. His only pleasure came from scheming to see Salma, but he never managed to pull that off in broad daylight. Everything he planned, or thought he had planned, failed to come to fruition; his were little more than the aimless intentions of a lovesick boy who was now twenty-five years old. But a string of coincidences confirmed he was on the right track and that she shared with him the anxieties of all young people in love.

Haleem Hammoud was celebrating that day. He had invited the people of the village over to mark his son's success in the primary-school examination, slaughtering two goats in his honour. The next morning he invited Abd al-Kareem for breakfast.

The food was little more than goat testicles and liver with two plates of salad made from cucumber, tomato, onion and mint. Abd al-Kareem wasn't hungry. His pain, which he couldn't hide from Haleem, had become unbearable. So he just sat there beside his friend and Haleem's five children.

Haleem's house was next to an ancient elevated stone courtyard. He claimed that his father had been killed on that wall thirty years ago fighting bandits who had come to steal their livestock. The thieves retaliated by destroying the southern part of the courtyard. Haleem had never got around to repairing it. Through the collapsed section that looked down on the agricultural road leading to al-Lajat, Abd al-Kareem saw Haleem's wife Mansoura gripping Salma's hand and dragging her inside against her will. Because the two of them were about the same height, they looked like sisters whenever they were together. He shivered with fright, and the food he was holding dropped from his hand.

The little conspiracy he found himself party to worried him, and he asked nervously, 'Have you and your wife come up with some kind of plan?'

'No, of course not!' Haleem swore before adding, to try to reassure Abd al-Kareem, 'Mansoura doesn't know a thing.'

They waited for the two women to come in. Abd al-Kareem was terrified to see Salma right there in front of him. He swayed as he got to his feet, and Haleem, sensing his discomfort, didn't get up, in order to avoid contact with a woman to whom he was not related. He had to greet her somehow, though, offering her his wrist so that he wouldn't soil her hand with the morsels of food still on his fingers. Mansoura busied herself in the kitchen, and scolded him without noticing that panic prevented him from moving or even saying a word. His ears started ringing, the bones in his skull were burning up, his body was slick with sweat and his heart began to pulsate like a motor. He pulled himself together with some difficulty just to avoid falling over.

The truth of the matter was that this wasn't happening the way he imagined meeting Salma in his dreams. In reveries, she was made of different stuff. And yet now here she was, just a few steps away, warm and close, full of vigour, soaked in the waters of life, spectral with light and shadows. He longed to touch her, to confirm she existed, to hear her voice, to utter just one kind word.

He muttered a few incomprehensible syllables and then waited, afraid of repeating the embarrassment of their previous encounter. It all nearly ended up the same way. The few moments after they had exchanged pleasantries and sat down were a mountain of unbearable silence.

But Haleem was an expert at breaking uncomfortable silences. He started talking right away, about everything, about nothing at all, the weather and the harvest, the children's accomplishments, Mansoura's bread, the aroma of boiled beef and mint, how far away the little boy was from the table. Haleem seemed so much in command as to be unstoppable – which was just what Abd al-Kareem needed. Now he realised why he loved Haleem so much. Thanks to him he was able to get control of his laboured breathing. He glanced at Salma, admiring all her attractive qualities, which he had tried not to think about during the past few days, now imagining what they might mean. It was as if she were an obscure dream carried along by the winds of youth, soaring like his heart. Yet now she was here, as clear and easy to read as a wondrous text containing all the secrets of creation, a mélange of rose extract and blossoms in her olive complexion. Even when she moved ever so slightly, he noticed how full her body was, how strong. And when the sunbeams streaming through the high window fell upon her he could feel her glowing, sparkling, illuminated like a firefly.

Encircled by a luminous halo, he imagined her to be an icon of the Virgin for a moment, but when she lowered her eyelids, concealing her beloved eyes from him, he got the feeling she had noticed his awkward silence, his breathless staring. It was the signal for him to come back down to earth. Nothing had changed. Haleem would talk; the two women would listen. He never failed to add a brief pause when changing the topic. He asked Salma how Saeed was doing, but she didn't respond right away, then quietly said that she hadn't heard anything from him for two months; he never wrote to her. Haleem said a man spends his entire life trying to please a woman.

'But travel doesn't please women,' Mansoura said.

'Just the opposite,' he said. 'There's nothing like travel to temper women's dreams with reality.'

'What about bachelors?' his wife asked him.

'They dream of satisfying a woman they haven't met yet.' Everyone had a good laugh. 'But what a devoted woman must never forget', he continued as Mansoura took his plate in order to refill it, 'is a man's stomach.'

They all laughed again. Salma's laugh was the loudest.

'Nothing empowers men quite like women's laughter,' Haleem commented.

'And their eyes, too,' Abd al-Kareem blurted out without thinking.

He could contain himself no longer. This encounter, charged with the energy of that radiant morning, had enervated him, changed his perception of things: food, home, friends. Salma was a vision of perfection. She made the world more bearable, the almost lyrical way she could make people laugh. A whole new hue was created out of her brilliant appearance, her stormy spirit, a kind of joy she wove from the threads of that silken moment, this unexpected meeting, a gift.

Rushing off towards the low clouds and the expansive fields, Salma would forget, moment by moment, the way home, if there even was a way home for her anymore. She was incapable of making a decision as simple as going home.

But now she could be sure about what had been troubling her: she was in love with him, as simple as that. All the doubts that had once plagued her, the states of denial, the mistrustful thoughts, deceptive, untrustworthy feelings now gone, from that moment forward, never to return.

By the time she finally left it was quite late already, almost noon. The day had grown much warmer, and nature was cloaked in dust. Far off in the valley she heard partridges chirping. She ran into a farmer who asked how her uncle was doing, and she told him he was out in the field. She forgot he had instructed her to bring his lunch down to him. Here was one of the disorientating aspects of her infatuation: forgetfulness.

Later, before Salma ever admitted to having a relationship with Abd al-Kareem, Sitt al-Husn said, 'She's acting the way lovers do.' Although she was suspicious of those feelings at first, Salma couldn't cure herself of this sickness. She became more and more afflicted by love.

When she first got back she didn't detect any reaction from Sitt al-Husn, who blamed the farmers for her being late, which was just as well for Salma. Hoping to placate her so-called mother-in-law she asked for some food and ate. She was surprised to discover that her appetite seemed to have no end, as though her stomach was empty. It was as if a spell had been cast upon her because it had only been half an hour since she had last eaten. Yet here she was, eating for a second time with the voraciousness of a shark. It was amazing to find such a variety of food here as well – *mujaddara*, salad and *laban* – she polished it all off. She would remember that day always. It would never happen again in the short time that remained of her life. In a state of wonder, she animatedly told Abd al-Kareem all about it during their first romantic encounter.

It was still unclear what was going to happen. Nearly all of her concerns from the previous few days had resurfaced. She had moved out of her uncle Sayyah's house, which had never offered her a safe haven where she could protect herself against whatever temptations might come her way. But she hadn't shown enough backbone – that is to say, she hadn't registered any opposition whatsoever to the paternalistic opinions her uncle had of her suitors.

Her life there had passed slowly. Time was repetitive and meaningless, without any memorable moments. She had lived in blind, artificial obedience to the orders and prohibitions of Sayyah Zeeb. Although her aunts and her uncle's wife had come to terms with their own lives – at least, that was the way it seemed to her – she and her cousin Naseeba found it impossible to understand the situation in which they found themselves. They completed all their chores without complaint: darning socks, hauling away the cattle dung, fetching water at dawn, using needle and thread to spruce up the furniture, pillowcases, curtains and sheets, whatever was deemed women's work. Neither one of them could understand the unchallengeable restriction that their uncle had imposed upon women's movement. They weren't allowed to attend village weddings. They knew only a small number of the residents even though the population wasn't all that large – this included their own relatives; the girls had heard the names of men and boys in the family from women who visited but they had only ever seen about half of them. But what they truly missed was attending the frequent funerals. The sole exception to Sayyah Zeeb's list of forbidden activities was going out to earn a wage.

Naseeba used to say that the women of the Zeeb family could only be saved by marriage or death. She wasn't joking; the idea had taken hold of her. When she began to think about it and to weigh her words more carefully, she came to believe that marriage was the root of all women's problems. She held fast to her position, refusing every proposal after Salma's death. For her part, Salma kept imagining the day she would be saved by marriage – even the word 'death' frightened her. But her wish didn't begin to take shape until she turned fifteen; it acquired definition as her desire for men was awakened, tinted by teenage dreams, the promise of a life free from the chains of her uncle's regime.

Time had taught her there were precious few opportunities in which she would be allowed to choose for herself. 'But how can I choose if I never meet anybody?' she asked Naseeba, ready to drink from the first glass offered to her.

She and Naseeba talked of marriage as if it were a new medical breakthrough, a dualistic, unpredictable glass of medicine that, with just one dose, could determine the fate of a miserably sick person facing death and ruin: either live with illness or end it all.

The ugly impression of men she had acquired from Sayyah was never far from her mind. She was melancholy and agitated. She thought she was ugly. Her intuition told her that escaping this deathly condition required nothing more than getting some fresh air out in the park or on the street. She paid no mind to what Naseeba said about men, going along with her uncle when he announced her engagement. What saddened her most, though, was that she didn't feel happy about it, just the opposite of what she would have expected. She looked out on her future as if she were standing on the edge of a deep gorge. What the bedroom held in store for her remained a secret that she would only discover in time.

There was a drought the year she got married. At first nature played a cat-and-mouse game. Then it rained for two days straight. When the rain finally stopped, the peasants planted their fields. But it didn't rain again. The sky cleared and the temperature rose. The sickly wheat and barley that had sprouted turned yellow, on the verge of dying. Then another disaster: the motor for the village well broke and the utilities agency was unable to fix it. The bureaucrat in charge claimed it needed parts that couldn't be found anywhere in the country; until a deal could be reached with some other country that made the parts they would just have to wait. It was like a curse, a grey tent made out of nature's darkness, a siege on everyday life. The earth started to crack open. What precious few sprouts of vegetation and fragile, tangled roots had managed to grow were soon devastated.

In April rats infested all the houses. Starving, emaciated creatures, chewing through furniture and clothing, pantries and empty sacks. Little children were terrified at the very sight of them. At just the right moment they would dart off with a piece of bread or a lump of cheese. The men tried to allay their fears by telling tales of famines past, but everyone shuddered at the thought that a year of pestilence could be upon them again. They had to buy everything. There was nothing to suggest that anything might change. Complaints from peasants were met with other complaints, no less tearful, from elected officials. Hysteria spread.

Salma had become used to having food delivered to her room on Sayyah Zeeb's instructions. But she was uncomfortable at what was happening all around her. She had to fight using all her powers of endurance under the new leadership of Sitt al-Husn. She wasn't allowed to have much of an opinion about anything, let alone the right to accept or change things. The first order of business was sending Salma to fetch water from the ancient well since the artesian well was out of commission. She had to walk more than two kilometres there and back just to get one bucket of water, and that was only enough for the house. Given all the chores – washing and dusting and feeding the animals – and how long it took to queue at the well, the only way to keep everything in order was for Salma to leave before 3 a.m. so she could collect three or four buckets before sunrise.

Throughout the day, Sitt al-Husn would come up with chores that kept Salma busy for hours at a time, preventing this young woman, whose dreams had been smashed by the hammer of false hope, from the physical ease that would have been her only possible respite and chance to mourn. Salma's strange silence, her dubious contentedness, her family's apparent abandonment of her – all these things bolstered Sitt al-Husn's power. She kept Salma as isolated as a wild dog that was being domesticated. What angered Sitt al-Husn most was the absolute certainty that Saeed was having sex with Salma every night. She would listen to the two of them, unable to breathe, through a crack she prised open in the shutter of the south-facing window of their room. When the two of them were done, she would cry and then go to sleep beside Abu Saeed's spent body, wracked with nausea and disgust. She would wake up in the morning filled with spite and the thirst for revenge.

The fact that Salma didn't even realise this weakened her ability to endure the pain until she simply couldn't take it any more. She complained to Saeed, but he responded with the insensitivity of a donkey, scoffing at her tears. 'Just try to get along with her. She's a good person.' She stopped trying to talk to him about it. In any case, she was sure that Saeed was no less hurt than she was by Sitt al-Husn's mood swings. She would later realise that this had been going on since the very beginning of their marriage.

On that first night, her dreams and reality collided when Salma willingly welcomed Saeed into her bed. He was as worked up as a raging bull. While he started to undress, she scrutinised him intently with a mixture of shame, acceptance and wonder. His body had been sculpted with the care of a master craftsman. Hairs were etched across his chest, pink as terracotta pottery, his waist taut as a bowstring. Saeed was well aware of this, and he proceeded to take his clothes off with macho pride, the cock of the walk. She was unable to continue looking at him once all his clothes were off, though. What transpired that first night was unlike what her aunts had told her would happen. As Saeed drew closer to her, swinging his lantern, he ordered her to take her clothes off as well. His voice was gravelly and deep, like a dry riverbed, and she submitted to him, giving up on the marital affection she had been led to hope for.

It all happened very quickly. Saeed performed deftly, without any games or foreplay. Without even waiting for her to get wet he entered her slowly, finishing with a brief fiery thrust, leaving behind a stinging memory and a bed spattered with her blood. Without kissing her even once, he got dressed and left.

Seconds later her aunt Umm Mut'ib came in and gave her a kiss, put her clothes back on and tucked her in before walking back out.

Everything seemed normal, carried on the shoulders of tradition, until Saeed returned to her room at the urging of Sitt al-Husn. Salma knew nothing about that until ten months later, after Umm Mut'ib told her. She hadn't understood what he was doing. She felt nauseous as she watched him get undressed this time. As he approached her everything about him seemed larger than life. She panicked and started to shake. She watched him coming towards her through the eyes of a little girl.

'For God's sake!' she pleaded with him meekly.

'What?' he demanded, angry and confused. Then he pinned her down like a butterfly and penetrated her, consummating the glory of his night once and forever.

She nearly bled to death.

From that point on Saeed had sex with her every night, all year long. During those first few months she came to hate the night-time, imagining she could postpone it somehow. Deep down in her heart she loathed sex, unable to comprehend how their relationship could consist of little more than the frenzied quenching of Saeed's desire. She started to believe that he hated her. He completely ignored her desires for intimacy. He believed that foreplay, caresses and any attempt to put a woman in the mood were things you only did with girlfriends. He did that with Sitt al-Husn, who repaid him with that first night's ambush and the unexpected sense of peace it brought about.

Ten months later there was nothing more Salma could do other than surrender to her husband in bed without even bothering to take off her clothes. It was better for her just to passively receive his manhood so that he would fall asleep satisfied. During the final months before he left he introduced a new ritual: forcing her to make dinner after every time they had sex. She had to accept the light being left on so there wouldn't be any uncertainty or doubt in the house. She would have expressed her hatred for him if he ever gave her the opportunity to do so. In the morning he was a different man altogether, eliciting outbursts of joy and laughter with an endless supply of jokes. After they had been married for ten months, without him once buying her a dress, a gown or even a nightshirt – he blamed that on poverty – she started to feel an intense affection for him. It was the first time she had ever felt that way, but she still didn't love him. She didn't hate him but she didn't love him either. She did everything she could to get rid of that tense atmosphere, beginning with her adjustment to Sitt al-Husn's strange habits, her surrender to Saeed's brazen desires and, finally, her silently joining with the villagers on those days spent praying for rain. The same way they prayed and chanted against the scarcity of rain, she prayed for her own private rain to fall, which she had been waiting for her entire life. But the sky didn't favour any of them. Neither of those rains ever came. The siege of sadness grew tighter, demolishing her last ramparts of hope.

In the second year of their marriage Saeed decided to go abroad.

He told her after climbing into bed. She couldn't believe it. Sitt al-Husn's terrorism was at an all-time high. She was sure that Saeed's departure would turn that woman into a demon. She didn't have any hard evidence of a secret relationship – although she had been worried about that – but Salma believed that she would be unable to stand up to her. As her fears became more pronounced, she frantically tried to persuade Saeed to stay. For the first time since they had married she was able to orgasm when they had sex. In the morning she realised that she was still clinging to childish fantasies. When he said goodbye to her fifteen days later she had no idea it would be the last time she would ever see him.

She found herself staring into a closed room, the boundaries of her life finally revealed to her, the charms of incarcerated beauty now outlined against the backdrop of an arid life, desiccated, a black curtain parched from drought, dreams like scrap metal, shattered jars, scattered pieces of straw and brittle grass.

She accepted her fate with stony resolve, understanding once she had contemplated the fates of those people all around her that hers was nothing but an exaggerated version of theirs. Her ordeal seemed like it would last an eternity. She was treated no better than a dog. This simplified impression was squeezed into the shadowy recesses of her mind, and she stubbornly held on to it like a little girl. Like a child she ignored simple twists of fate. In the glorious rear-view mirror she hadn't been able to escape Abd al-Kareem's eyes, flush with questions and contemplation, brimming with desire. She couldn't believe this was love; she hadn't been expecting it. From the day she met him at Haleem's house she had been sure she would never be able to return along the unknown road she had started down. She resented the life she had lived up until that point, the dark stream of difficulties, that strange amalgam of frustration and obedience. She was determined to raise her fist and chart a new course. She resolved to get there, to think for herself, to find strength in all the things that could be found on a path leading to him, unfettered by hidebound tradition that required a man to take the first step.

But the changing circumstances as well as her environment, a space too small for the initiatives of a woman in love – the fear of being found out and the uncertainty of the future – made her failures and false starts look more like the actions of a dazed partridge. But there were a few events, inspired by the torrent of their love, that provided shelter for the seed of their relationship. In the end it turned out to also be the fruit of their transgressions, experiments and schemes to which they dedicated themselves with the enthusiasm and sincerity of children.

That unforgettable summer day. The village was typically warm for that time of year. Since morning it had been obvious what was going to happen. The sky was filled with dazzling sunshine, a mirage-like haze on the horizon. Silence fell over the road and the alleyways, the gardens and forests. By late morning there were no traces of living creatures, opening up a space of emptiness, strangeness, everything seemingly set to ignite. In the afternoon the village was caked in nature's ruin, locked in the suffocating mountain heat. It wasn't until evening that a few milder winds started to blow, making the air slightly less unbearable. After dinner more than half the village attended the al-Hasan family's wedding, not only out of affection or the joyousness of the occasion but also because of the desire to be liberated from that stifling heat.

That was where they met.

She wanted to turn straight back around as soon as she saw him. She lingered for a few seconds, though, pretending to wait for a friend, watching him out of the corner of her eye. In her youthful excitement she thought he hadn't noticed her. But he didn't come to the wedding without first making sure, by way of secret investigations and the extensive interrogation of his sister and his cousins, that she would actually be there. He nearly gave himself away. He did his best not to be seen when he first arrived, skulking in the shadows of the thick oak trees, away from the noise of the revellers. He crossed the side road running along the riverbed, hiding himself behind a dilapidated building for a moment before darting towards the path to Mahmoud Hasan's house so that when he arrived it would seem as if he had just been passing through the neighbourhood. At almost that exact moment he glimpsed two figures in the shadow of the building locked in an embrace. At first he thought they were just mirages of love but the man jumped out of the darkness, then ran away and disappeared, the woman frozen in fear. Abd al-Kareem could hear her weeping but didn't turn towards her. He didn't recognise her.

That was the first hiccup in his plan, but he tried to put it to one side even as the woman's crying pierced his heart. The second came when he saw three women accompanying Salma as she left the wedding. He had assumed – he had no clue where he got the idea – that she would go home alone. After seeing that group of people, he briefly considered calling off his plan to confess his love to her. But an invisible force – perhaps it was a wave; maybe it was a particle – drove him to follow the women slowly, disoriented by the crowds of people, the herds of children, the groups of young men and women. He was mesmerised by Salma's tremulous eyes, nervous in this climate of fear that he might have to talk to her while others were around, even if she tried to slip away from them. It was a kind of determination he hadn't expected, but he understood her the way love demanded. It was a wilful invitation for him to proclaim his love for her.

He would do just that. He began to retrace his steps and the path of his return. In that moment she walked in front of Nawwaf's house, past Ra'uf's windows, then came down the street alone. She stumbled across the rubble of Salman's crumbling wall, leaping over it like a gazelle, clearly in a hurry. Why was she in such a rush? Was she about to vanish? Was he going to lose his chance? Act now or you'll never be able to say hello, Abd al-Kareem. He jogged after her. It drove him crazy to see her dart down a narrow alleyway, heading for home.

She had been waiting for him!

She walked slowly, dripping with sweat from the panic and confusion as well as the heat. She could sense his light, quick footsteps, like a bird following just behind her. She wished she had had more romantic experience so that she could contribute something to the courage that drove him forward. But her beauty alone gave him enough confidence to keep going ... until he was right behind her. She stopped and turned around to see that he was trembling, unable to look straight at her, aimless. They stood there for a few seconds, listening to the sound of their lovesick breathing.

'Good evening,' he mumbled with affection.

'Good evening to you,' she said kindly, blinking her eyes.

'Where are you coming from?' he asked.

'Heaven,' she replied. 'And you?'

'Earth.'

They laughed as one. His confusion lifted. Life was rekindled deep down inside of him.

'Did you enjoy the wedding?' he enquired.

'Not so much.'

'Why not?'

'I don't like all the commotion.'

'You prefer quiet?'

'Naturally.'

'Me too.'

'I know.'

'You know? Who told you?'

'The birds.'

'What else did they tell you?'

'I forget.'

'Will you remember tomorrow maybe?'

'Maybe.'

'I'll see you tomorrow then, so you can tell me?'

'Sure.'

'Great.'

'Where should we meet?'

'In the orchard behind our house, by the olive tree.'

'What time?'

'A little after ten.' Then she turned around and walked towards her house.

On the way back, he got the feeling that someone was following him. His suspicions were confirmed when he changed his route and spotted a woman trying to keep up with him. With the temper of a child, he thought about stopping and screaming in her face to get away from him. He felt like he was being hunted. He wanted to tell her there was no room right now for another woman in his heart where an image of Salma had been embroidered but he thought better of such childish talk. The woman's footsteps were getting closer still. She was speeding up, apparently trying to catch up with him. When she called out his name he stopped. As she drew closer he saw who it was.

'Suad? Everything all right?'

Suad's face flashed with anger, like a double-edged blade. 'Don't think for a second I don't know what's going on! I saw the two of you together. Come on, tell me everything!'

He was stunned. His knees felt like they would buckle. Unable to stand, he braced himself against the nearest wall. His blood ran cold. He thought about making her swear to God she would keep her mouth shut or else he would strangle her right there and then but she didn't give him the chance. She was bitter and outraged, unable to keep up the act.

She started to cry, giving up whatever glory she had achieved in her stealth attack just a moment before. She told him she was at his disposal – to protect his secret, to be his messenger to Salma, to pass along to her whatever information he wanted.

When he asked her the reason for this change of heart, in flustered disbelief at what he was hearing, she replied, on the brink of collapse, 'Don't make me tell you.'

The whole situation was ridiculous. She could have

taken advantage of him. And yet Abd al-Kareem accepted her offer. He wanted to tell her he didn't intend to do anything inappropriate, that he didn't want to have a clandestine relationship. But making this public would have to wait. Amid the endless torments of his infatuation, the idea that this woman, who was so panicked by the scandal of it all, could help service the relationship was too good an opportunity to pass up.

His conscience wouldn't have allowed him to take advantage of her vulnerability like that had it not been for the rock-solid assurance he received from her that she understood he wasn't blackmailing her; rather, they were both offering a reciprocal favour – discretion.

Other than that, he felt deep affection for her. When he saw the man she had been with, he was sure that her tryst had nothing to do with the kind of love he and Salma had forged.

Suad was the most infamous spinster in town. She had been rebuffing suitors since before she turned twenty, claiming that none of them were worthy of her beauty, the charms she had recognised in herself early on. Then misfortune befell her. She had always rejected young men who were interested in her by way of a strange, silent and undeclared covenant. Abd al-Kareem couldn't understand why, even though scores of men and women had given their own colourful interpretations. As she got older, Suad became willing to accept any man, only to change her mind once again to absolute rejection after thirty. Every time a suitor was fought off, the fate she had sealed for herself made it hard for her to sleep.

She didn't lose her allure as she got older. She remained capable of provoking gasps of distress and regret whenever she made her way down the street or bumped into a group of men. When she found out that some schoolchildren had started calling her 'the Eternal Spinster', she was crushed with sorrow – and yet somehow she had also acquired another nickname, 'Merry Suad'. They told her that both names had been taken from the title of a book that they had to study in eighth grade about Marie Curie, the Eternal Student. She vowed to hold on to that nickname no matter what. But the needs of the body are indifferent to the vows of the mind. If she had been able to withstand their cruelty with the occasional small victory, the arrival of her aunt's husband Salman brought down all of her defences. Her promise had been broken. Eventually she raised the white flag, after persistent assaults on her weakness and vulnerability took advantage of her inclination towards infidelity, a well-known weapon in her arsenal.

It had been her idea to arrange a meeting during the wedding. That was one of the most telling signs of her inexperience. Salman tried to persuade her otherwise but she insisted, arguing that the noise of the singers and the fact that everyone would be distracted would keep their rendezvous a secret. That same stubbornness drove her to follow Abd al-Kareem. She cried when she saw him meet up with Salma.

She was supposed to have kept herself out of sight – she concluded later – but she didn't. She didn't regret it, though. Abd al-Kareem kept his promise and she kept hers. She remained the anonymous cupid that brought those infamous lovebirds together, forever unknown.

Her proposition was a good omen. Salma had already broken the first commandment of love. Sitt al-Husn's illness was her first obstacle – she had come down with a severe throat infection after leaving the bakery the night before, feverish from the combination of the heat of the oven and the warm weather, her body radiating. After a bath, she felt pain in her temples, and weakness forced her to sit down. In a panic, she gripped Salma's hand, convinced that she was going to die. As her throat got increasingly painful and her voice went hoarse, Salma could no longer remain calm and obedient. She felt as if she were about to be slaughtered, that a crown of blood would be constructed out of Sitt al-Husn's bones. When she saw her eating vigorously to stave off death from this illness, Salma became despairingly certain that this was a sign that she would recover, and that the gates of her own life had been shut by Sitt al-Husn's sneaky ruses.

But her feelings of trepidation evaporated the following day, which she spent trying to work out another way to meet up with Abd al-Kareem. Suad showed up that evening. The spinster came to visit for the first time in a long while in order to bring a message while doing her best not to arouse any suspicions. She had to be patient, to have faith in the courage she had gained since Abd al-Kareem confided in her. She carried out her mission deftly and subtly, convinced that any funny stuff at this point would only be an insult to their love. Salma savoured the words of the message, which were perfumed with lustful desire. She wasn't afraid of what lay in store, didn't have time to worry about that.

After Suad left, Salma was burning up, her whole body quivering with anticipation. Even though the message Suad had delivered left her feeling nervous, she didn't miss their ten o'clock appointment, getting herself ready in a state of rapturous excitement.

She planned to wear a nightgown when she went to see Sitt al-Husn, give her some food and then settle her in. She shut the door loudly enough for Abu Saeed to hear. But edginess made her open the door again and go out to get a drink, come back and close it, then open it once more, causing her uncle to call out to ask what she was up to.

'Nothing,' she squeaked in fear. She went back inside, putting a stop to her foolish behaviour. She stood by the window, waiting until it was time, looking out at the courtyard that was bathed in a pale hazy light.

She couldn't behave any other way. She found herself looking forward to her rendezvous with the excitement of a lonely woman whose bad luck was finally coming to an end. Here she was, on the cusp of twenty years of age, believing for the first time in her life that she was actually alive, that her heart was beating, that there was an infinite number of things in this world to love. When she related all of this to Abd al-Kareem he told her there was no need to regret anything that had happened in the past, that bringing up past trials and tribulations would only stifle their love.

She respected his advice but felt that taking this at face

value would unnecessarily subject her further to the vagaries of fate.

'Maybe I can't forget anything,' she said miserably.

'Why not?'

'I don't know.'

She found it difficult to get over life's twists and turns. Abd al-Kareem tried to cheer her up but all he could come up with was a naïve and half-baked suggestion that they gaze up at the moon together. It was an off-the-cuff suggestion, made even stranger by the cloudiness of that tranquil night. Salma acquiesced, gazing upwards with mournful eyes.

As her memories started to accumulate, she said, 'When I was little, the moon was my only friend. The light from the gas heater used to frighten me when I went to sleep. I'd stare up at the ceiling and watch countless shadows and ghosts: tall, wide and round. One time, I shrieked when I saw a large figure floating towards me, its mouth wide open. I hadn't realised that my mother had got up to bring me a glass of water, and it was her shadow moving towards me along the wall in the shape of a monster.'

'I've been that scared before.'

'Ever since then, all I've had is the moon.'

'Now, tell me truthfully, who do you like better, me or the moon?'

She laughed and hugged him.

They spent their first night together struggling to feel their way around one another. As he listened to the sound of her voice, harmonious as a flute, Salma's spring-like colours dazzled Abd al-Kareem, and it was all he could do just to hold her in his arms, to protect her. She yearned to embrace him with a lover's passion.

The stance he took wasn't for any lack of love but rather on account of his tremendous moral strength. He couldn't think of any other way to prove his love to her. The Platonic ideal of love that inspired him was exemplified by his unwavering commitment not to bring sex into the relationship at this stage. It wasn't an act. His resolve was so strong and so true that she was able to draw strength from his desire. He believed that not holding back from sex would be a mistake that might destroy their love. Even though he was rock solid in his commitment to this decision, to the point of piety, the power of love compelled him to kiss Salma again and again without any sexual connotations.

The first time he kissed her, it was a vision of their new life together. After their initial encounter she had been certain he didn't love her. She hadn't expected anything to happen, but afterwards she would think about how if he had tried to sleep with her during their first encounter she wouldn't have said no. He didn't, however. She surrendered to his way of being without fully understanding it, without finding a reasonable way to make him change his mind or give him the green light to make a physical advance. During their first few meetings his approach made her feel silly. It wasn't that she was desperate to sleep with him but that she feared something about the situation would push Abd al-Kareem away from her so she doubled her efforts to make herself pretty before their dates. She bathed each and every time, changed her underwear, brushed her teeth with sugar, washed her hands with scented soap several times and spritzed perfume under her arms. She didn't put on foundation, though, because Abd al-Kareem once told her that women's faces slathered with makeup reminded him of dead people.

Nevertheless, he still would not look at her as if he desired her physically. There was no specific aspect of her beauty that stirred up his love for her. It was distance, a windy and rainy sky bursting with passionate love. Every time they got together he would take her to new places in their fields of love: the great biographies of lovers, love stories, tales of repression and revolution. He was encouraged further by her wonder, her questions about the new life opening up before them. He started to explain his political hopes and dreams of justice. Then he told her about the various films he had seen in Beirut and Damascus. She may have only understood a fraction of what he was trying to tell her but his love was being planted like a tree in her soul. His branches broke through here and there. The more she dedicated herself to solitude, distancing herself from the impression of men she had acquired from Sayyah Zeeb and Saeed Kharsan, the deeper those roots grew into her. When it became possible, they plunged into her soil.

After every meeting she would remain awake until morning, patiently redrawing the details in her mind – his face, his movements, his words – colouring the images with the hues of flawless memory. Then she would fall asleep, traces of happiness on her lips that had come down from the endless sky of love.

After he wrote her his first love letter she blossomed. She

chirped like a little bird when he told her how ridiculous it had seemed a few days earlier that he would even think about asking his mother to see if he could get engaged to Salma. He was unable to resist the burning desire to kiss her. Salma tasted of ripe grapes and sweet water in that fleeting, warm kiss. She was embarrassed by his impetuous courage but she did nothing to slow him down for even a moment in order to reflect on the situation, bursting forth in an explosive fit of repressed desire and love, kissing him all over his face, tears streaming from her eyes. Her rains had arrived at long last.

They walked up their path several times. But the distant horizon they gazed upon together was hazy, unknown, shrouded in oblivion. Where were they headed? And what after that? The sky was no help to them. The weather had turned following fifteen days of scorching heat. Beads of dew appeared all around, and the peasants started getting ready to go out for the harvest once again. That night, from ten o'clock onwards, the fields were filled with lanterns and the folk songs of the harvesters.

Then there was a cold spell. If they were going to shelter themselves from the hail they couldn't meet where they did usually. Every time she got ready to say goodbye she would gaze at him in the milky glow of that June evening, covered in white clouds, illuminated by moonlight. He couldn't believe it. She was like a dream lying there beside him, alive, glowing with love for him. He felt a kind of splendour. He was loved. She hurried to meet him every night, an amazing woman full of passion, as hot as fire, as fertile as a rain-fed year.

It was only in that moment that his murky thinking over the past few days coalesced into a decision. He saw it across the dirty surface of the sky, mapped out in radiant lines, as if it had been written up there for all eternity. His heart quickened, wouldn't settle down. His teeth started to chatter, his body tensed under a weight of anticipation that pressed down upon him suddenly, drenching his body in a river of sweat. Then, with no warning, without understanding why, he knew with the conviction of a prophet that if he didn't deliver his message now he would never be able to tell her. He realised he couldn't live without Salma. He had overcome all the obstacles, and what he was about to say would tear down the last barrier standing in the way of his love. The only thing holding him back was his fear that she would reject him.

But she didn't. Instead she confounded him with a strange answer to his proposal.

As she tried to get up he took her hand and asked in a tender voice, 'Salma?'

'Yes, my love.'

'Will you marry me?'

She perked up, as excited as a dove. She was bewildered by this unexpected turn of events, this sign of glad tidings.

He heard a distant voice, pounding with strength, a clamour deep down inside.

'You're crazy,' she said, staring back at him.

'I'm not.'

'You want us to run off together?'

'Let's run away together, Salma. We'll just run away.'

'And live together for ever?'

'That's right.'

'And I'll have your son?'

'A daughter, like you.'

'A son would be better.'

'And the girl will be as delicate as a leaf.'

'So we can spoil her.'

'Her father would never do that.'

'Do you know something, Abd al-Kareem? Some days I tell myself I've loved you for a long time, since before I ever laid eyes on you.'

'Ever since you were a little girl?'

'That's right.'

'It's so strange! Why did it have to take so long for us to find this kind of happiness?'

'Maybe God loves us after all.'

'Yes, perhaps he does.'

'Once, when I was a little girl, my cousins and I went out on the main road. We listened to the sounds coming up out of the belly of the earth. It was like magic. Nobody knew where they were coming from. Anyway, it made you feel like you were in heaven or flying through the air. Naseeba said they were the sounds of the *djinn* underground, that they were having a wedding. Hind said no, it's the sound of cars, far, far away on the Damascus road, travelling to other countries. Ever since that day I've dreamed about going away in a car, about disappearing somewhere nobody can find me. When I first saw you, I said, that's him, and here's our car. I'd go anywhere with you!'

She was pleading with him. Her voice reverberated like a flute. That image, fuelled with longing, only increased

Abd al-Kareem's excitement, driving him to take the most important step of his life, the decision to end their encounter. An idea flashed through his mind – the big decisions we take in such troubled times seem more decisive the longer it has been since we made them. Because of his intense joy, he believed Salma might change her mind or else create difficulties or alert him to some danger. So in response he simply said goodbye to her, satisfied, his mind at peace.

On his way home he nearly gave himself away. He stumbled when he tried to hop over the wall of Abu Daoud's orchard. Cobbled together out of medium-sized stones and assorted junk, the wall collapsed with a loud crash. He leaped out of sight, trying to avoid the bright torchlight someone aimed in his direction from a rooftop on the other side of the street. A watchman patiently inspecting what might have caused the collapse.

The mishap only strengthened his resolve. He never once thought about the obstacles in their way – not then and not any other time – nor about what misfortunes their risky behaviour could cause. He realised that he possessed all the powers that he needed: chivalry, vigour, the impulsiveness of those who are in love.

Salma had been just as enthusiastic but her determination was now giving out as she lay in her bed. Debilitating anxieties ran through her head. She couldn't sleep. She was well aware of the fact that, as a woman, she had far greater obstacles to overcome than Abd al-Kareem. And even if her rational mind couldn't make those calculations, her feelings, intuition and her very existence all made her understand what was at stake.

As she contemplated her situation she realised that extricating herself from all the shame and agony, the deadly knives of tradition, would require as much energy as an erupting volcano. She would have to keep this sudden panic to herself, this fear of her family and the growing feeling that she was doing something wrong, if she was going to make her dreams come true.

In feverish moments of despair she nearly changed her mind, but the pull of hope was too strong; her love propelled her towards the promise of happiness.

The only thing that could get in her way was the conflict brewing inside of her. She would send Saeed a message, asking for a divorce. It seemed like a reasonable idea to her at the time, as she struggled to eliminate the unhappiness in her life, but her mind had to make other calculations. How long would it take for the letter to arrive? How long would it take for him to get back to her? And what would she do if Saeed were to come back?

Would he ever?

She had no shortage of doubts. The spectre of a terrible misfortune loomed in her dreams in the form of a twisted structure topped with ruined domes, glimpsed through a fog. She would watch for the early warning signs of her life to come, warm sunny visions, the ship for her voyage beaming rays of light into the deep white void, the captain raising the anchor. She pushed away her sorrowful decision, letting go of a passing fancy that was now poisoned, ecstatic with the renewed promise of permanent happiness.

She had stayed up late, past midnight, when her uncle

Sayyah's faint knock came to wake her so she could get ready for the harvest. She pretended to have been asleep, answering him in a groggy voice, even though there was no need for her to do so. Her uncle was fast sliding towards senility and would never have noticed anything anyway. Besides, he had enough to worry about with what Sitt al-Husn had piled on top of him to distract him from this world. But Salma wasn't thinking about that. The mind of a child grew inside of her. She became convinced that her thoughts were being communicated to her uncle, under the ground, up in the sky, through the wheat fields. All he had to do was read the signs and he would discover everything.

These were wild delusions. Sayyah walked all over his large shadow, elongated on the ground by the floodlights, without saying a word. Salma walked behind him, noting how his short, stooped body had been weighed down by the burdens of age and life. In the throes of her excitement she thought for an instant about revealing her secret to him. He would be sure to forgive her. He might even help. She didn't, though. Obsessive thoughts had scrambled her brain and sapped her strength, hung her on a pendulum as she anxiously anticipated what was going to happen. Now she was going to escape the tomb of her tortuous and punishing thoughts. She had no other choice. To hell with them. Happiness shouldn't be kept a secret. Life's green horizons signalled that she should throw herself into the company of the young man who she wished had come into her life much earlier.

She recognised that this is the way life goes. If she were to be happy she would have no choice but to burn the firewood of worries and sorrow. This brilliant idea put an end to her pangs of conscience. When the harvest began she crouched down on her knees until morning without standing up once, unaffected by the rocks and thorns, sailing on the waves of dewy straw without a care in the world. Her uncle was impressed with this remarkable display of hard work. The approaching holiday helped her to overlook the fact that she was running herself ragged during the harvest.

She would never forget that night. When the others brought it up later, as they passed by the field, she knew her life was over. She was like a crop for the scythe, only her wheat was inedible.

Their rendezvous was scheduled for the following night. At first Abd al-Kareem was unable to come up with a practical plan for their elopement. His original idea was as simple as black and white. They would take the winding road, making a big semi-circle before reaching the main road. But the field would be covered with lights and farmers all evening, which made his plan impossible. In any other circumstance he would likely have called the whole thing off, but he didn't. Despite the pessimism and obsessiveness that were distracting him, his mind – or his madness, as he later told himself – led him to a different conclusion. He got to it right away, even though he realised that its success would require uncommon luck or the kind of power that could draw blood from a stone. Salma supported the proposition with adventurous delight. They had carved out a path together and they would walk down it together, getting through the terrifying moments and hard times.

Their plan was to pass right through the heart of the village, shielded by the groups of farmers who rarely noticed anything so late at night. Instead of finding each other further down the road, they would meet up in a cave they had both heard about, although neither had ever been there.

As they got closer Abd al-Kareem squeezed Salma's arm with encouragement, whispering confidently, 'Don't be afraid.'

Once they had made it through safely and she saw the car there waiting for them, she exclaimed, 'I thought you might have brought me a white horse!'

It was a wonderful image. He didn't know whether she said that to bring him joy or to describe her own but he knew it would be his most cherished memory. He would remember this well after she was dead, plagued with crushing regret for not having actually done it. Their elopement was the last night they would ever see one another.

The man who hosted them offered Salma a bed in a room she would share with his two daughters while he slept with Abd al-Kareem in the guest room.

At first he thought the situation wouldn't last more than one night. They were too young to be bothered by tradition, the very last entry in the lovers' lexicon. But now tradition was leaping to the preface, setting the scene for the collapse of their lovers' dream to be chronicled in the very first chapter.

Abd al-Kareem couldn't sleep. He was so close to Salma, separated by only a few metres. He didn't regret anything, dreaming of tomorrow and tomorrow alone.

News of their misfortune came in the morning. Abu Nayef, the owner of the house, declared that he and Salma could not sleep in the same room together. His voice was dry, as if wafting out of a crypt, his eyes dark and his sallow face was the colour of ash. He said he wouldn't give them sanctuary. When Abd al-Kareem tried to explain their situation, their host said he had no respect for elopers. These words were poison. This was not what Abd al-Kareem had expected. Why hadn't he thought it might come to this, though? Haleem had said this was the only man capable of protecting them. The way Haleem had talked about Abu Nayef should have been a red flag.

'What are we supposed to do?' he asked. 'I love her, and she loves me. We want to be together.' He would have continued talking, painting for this man the rose-tinted portrait of a future they imagined for themselves placed in a frame decorated with daisies and anemones, with the intermingled details of their home together, children and long years that would run over with happiness, safe harbours, forests snowed under with nourishing nectar.

But Abu Nayef had another reaction altogether: he grabbed his pistol and loaded it noisily, raving, 'I could protect the both of you against a danger as large as a mountainside, but I'll be damned if I'm gonna let any creature alive call me a pimp.'

Abd al-Kareem stared back at him. His eyes roved over the gargantuan head of this fifty-something man, his fingers as thick as a cane, his wheat-coloured skin, his face darkened like a mask. This wasn't the same man who had greeted them the night before: a different sort of Bedouin guardian angel, welcoming, sowing the seeds of tranquillity in their nervous hearts.

'He's like a horse,' Salma had described him in a whisper.

The pistol was still in Abu Nayef's hand, but to Abd al-Kareem's powerless, paralysed astonishment his features relaxed into kindness and mercy.

Putting his hand on Abd al-Kareem's shoulder, he said, 'Don't be upset. Whoever throws off his robe is bound to get cold, am I right? Well, this is our robe, the traditions of our forefathers. What'd you expect from me? Your bride is yours. Get her out of my hair!'

He put his gun back in its holster under his armpit.

All of a sudden the conversation returned to the severity of the drought. Abd al-Kareem re-created the situation with the brushstrokes of a painter bleaching out the yellow and the dryness, filling in its cracks with grasses, watering it as if in an imaginary world, constructing it out of dreams and magic and folk-tales. He was going to freeze. Exposure would consume him. The warmth of those traditions lurking inside Abu Nayef would be the end of him. But he gambled one last time on whatever words he had up his sleeve.

'We got married just a couple days ago, Abu Nayef.'

'Fantastic. Why'd you come to me, then?'

'Some people told me that you're the only who can help us sort things out.'

'Sort things out? Sure. But the two of you aren't going to sleep in the same room before that.'

Two days later Abu Nayef was invited over to Sayyah

Zeeb's. Sayyah acted like a wounded wolf, didn't pay attention to what was said, angrily muttering instead.

'So she's at your place!' He said that and nothing else, nothing more than an outraged exclamation about Salma's whereabouts emerging from the depths of his spite. He was falling apart, cracked open like the earth. And in violation of tradition he stormed out of the parlour, abandoning his guest there in shock and disappointment.

Instead of waiting until morning to head over to the county seat he set out straight away. He intended to take advantage of his friendship with the county chief as soon as possible. They were about the same age, and this public servant, who had attained the rank of distinguished officer twenty-five years earlier, found in Sayyah a true friend whenever he wasn't carrying out his professional responsibilities. When Salma ran away he was the first to hear Sayyah's grumbling and his pain. But now Sayyah was seeing red, as boughs of revenge dangled over him. He didn't hide his elation over the discovery of her whereabouts.

'I found her!' he told the county chief as soon as he saw him.

The chief would have laughed at this overexcitement had it not been for his deep understanding of what the whole situation meant. The two of them went inside to have some coffee. The chief seemed nervous, moving awkwardly, carefully pretending to be oblivious to Sayyah's problem.

'Everything all right, Abu Hisham?' he asked.

'Just fine,' the chief replied, sipping his coffee in a daze. 'Sayyah Bey,' he said, slowing things down a bit, 'your wish is my command, but I need you to promise me something.'

'At your service, Abu Hisham.'

He was ready to do whatever the chief asked of him. He was exhausted by everything that had happened. It had sapped his strength, sent him tumbling into the abyss of scandal. He had been worn down by hardship, had turned as black as ashes and was sagging like an overburdened donkey. In his heart, deep down in an undiscovered part of his body, a state of grief emerged that forced his head down and bent his back. While he had hoped for a wind that could blow away his bone-chilling problems, it was turning out to be little more than a gentle breeze. The chief had his concerns, too. He saw clearly what was happening: they were going to kill Salma as soon as she was brought back. They might kill Abd al-Kareem as well. This idea stopped him in his tracks because of the professional humiliation it would cause.

The sun had already set when he looked out the window. Olive trees in the courtyard of the house he was renting swayed in the breeze. He was nervous, stumbling more than once as he walked out of the room.

Finally, he turned to Sayyah and said, 'I know you're a man, so promise me you're going to protect her life. Don't kill her! If you promise me that, you'll have her back in a few days.'

Sayyah stood up to move towards him, shook his hand and grunted, 'Take a few days, but know this: I am going to kill her with my own two hands.'

Once he was far enough away he spat on the ground and snarled hatefully, 'I'm going to kill her even if all the prophets are on her side!'

☪

'Kill me first,' Abu Nayef said to the police the next day. 'Kill me, just don't take her from my house.' His voice was shrouded in sorrow. 'What will I say to the mountainside? How will I ever be able to face anyone again?'

The chief assured him that they weren't going to kill her, and that neither was he. Then he ordered him to bring her out. 'Hurry up!' He wanted to be done with this case.

She hadn't waited around for them to arrive. She and Abd al-Kareem had spent three hours together the day before. And just like that her hope turned to despair.

The next few days were all murk and darkness. With heavy hearts they received the news that Sayyah had ruled out any attempt at mediation. The misery of the preceding days only amplified their gloom. But the two of them managed to reunite at last. It was Abu Nayef himself who facilitated the meeting, sensing that he was only offering temporary reprieve from a future payment.

They lay down, curled up next to each other without speaking for a few minutes, locked in an embrace and each listening to the beating of the other's heart. She was trembling, defeated ever since she heard about the rage that consumed Sayyah. She might have expected this, but she had forgotten all about him amid their plans to run away. All that there was left of him for her were disturbing memories, dark and shadowy sadness. He had come back to haunt her mind, her soul, her frail and tender body, her memory that was like an overgrown forest. She was intimidated, but Abd al-Kareem beat back her panic with his optimism, which seemed to overpower everything else.

'Everything's going to be fine,' he said, holding her close. 'What do we do now?'

She didn't know. The possibility of separation was what troubled her most. If she could sacrifice herself to protect him she would do it, but she would never accept any power on earth that forced them to live apart from one another.

Just then she took his face in her hands, looked him square in the eyes and then walked over to the window. As she swept aside the curtains the room was illuminated with a stunning, warm light. She stood there for a moment, staring at him, then drew closer and got down on her knees in front of him. None of this made any sense: her clumsy movements and dreamy gaze, this maddening silence with her eyes wide open like windows, her body in motion. But he knew what was happening, may have known about it for a very long time, since before he had been born, in a past life. He saw her, and she saw him, pledged to one another.

'You know something? I realise now that I've never seen your face in the daylight, never really looked at you. Let me look at your face a little longer.'

Her face seemed to brim with restrained passion, like rainclouds in the morning. It was as if that secret, the inferno of his love, only heightened her adolescent enthusiasm. Just then he was seduced by an idea that hardened into a conviction that Salma might for eternity be able to give him the love he had always lacked. She might allow him to blissfully forget all his bitterness. Was this a wave of calm washing over him? Superstition? A kind of superstition they believed in together, one that united them, which they had chosen, which they constructed out of ships and mornings and roses? Unfortunately, they had both forgotten about the thorns.

She looked like a tree to him, wispy, tremulous, on the verge of splitting open. She deserved nothing less than love, winged love delivered by lightning, wrapped in joy. But a year later, when he thought back on these moments, he realised how blind he had been: how could he have failed to notice the saffron twilight spreading through her eyes? Much later his mother would say it was the colour of death.

'Salma!' he cried. 'What should I buy for you? I haven't bought anything yet. What do you want? Tell me!'

The idea stunned her. She held up her ruined lilac dress and cried, 'Look! My dress is torn. I don't have another one. It's been two years since anyone bought me a new dress.' She was ashamed as she realised that her words conveyed more complaint than love, but it didn't seem to bother him, and he proceeded to list all the things he was going to buy for her the next day.

'Three shawls and a white dress, a new shirt, underwear, a woollen sweater for the coming winter, shoes, slippers, two green necklaces, trousers to wear out for picnics.'

He bought her everything he had promised, without exception, frittering away all the money he had with the heedlessness of someone head over heels in love. But she wasn't there when he got back.

She wasn't waiting around for them to find her; she had been waiting for him. When she handed him a lock of her hair, she screamed, 'Take it!' Once he had done so, she whispered, 'Now I understand. You want to come back to me.' Her mind was a time capsule. She imagined him coming back bearing gifts from exotic streets in joyous celebration, bearing lanterns – sights she hadn't seen since she was a child.

Ever since he left that morning she had been counting the minutes that never seemed to end. From the start time grew taut, tense. After only an hour she was filled with regret for agreeing to let him go.

She was worried about him, worn down by premonitions and hallucinations. She didn't fall asleep until morning, finally freeing herself from the grip of that desolate time that awaited her, besieging her. She didn't wake up until Abu Nayef knocked on the door of her room, bringing word of her impending death.

Moments like ashes!

Drawing in towards her, Abu Nayef was like a stone, rolling along with disappointment and feelings of defeat. His hand trembled, his heart fluttered, stilled like a docile rabbit by Sayyah Zeeb, who had got him into this mess in the first place. In his eyes Salma was innocent, as pure as a covenant. He realised that this man might be the harbinger of her death but he didn't really believe that the threats from such an erratic person could actually harbour such violence. Then he told her the police were coming to take her away.

She whirled around towards him, petrified, and said, with a spite he would never forget, 'Have you no decency?'

He fell to the ground, wounded. When he finally pulled himself together, he asked her, 'Do you know where they're going to take you?'

She nodded her head several times, muttering, 'Yes. To my death.'

'So hurry up then!' he barked in a hollow voice, turning around to leave.

All alone now, she could no longer put up any kind of fight. Her energy had been sapped during this losing battle. Bad timing. She felt as though she were disappearing even as she watched herself drift into that terrifying darkness. She started to shiver, overcome momentarily, her body bathed in an icy sweat. When she finally snapped out of it she had become a new woman. She wouldn't surrender – this was her decision. There was no going back, from that moment until her death, murdered in the horse shed, with Jamil Zeeb's delirious shouting ringing in her ears:

Die!

Die!

Die!